———◆———

BUCHANAN'S SIEGE

———◆———

by
Jonas Ward

A FAWCETT GOLD MEDAL BOOK

Fawcett Publications, Inc., Greenwich, Conn.

BUCHANAN'S SIEGE

August 1973

BUCHANAN'S SIEGE

1

Tom Buchanan rode outside on the stage mainly because they had not built a Conestoga suitable to his six-foot-four, two-hundred-and-forty-pound frame, but also because he had not been in big-sky country for some years and wanted to enjoy the view. They were coming onto the plain toward Buffalo with green graze all around in early summer, trees luxurious along the road, cattle waxing fat, produce now growing where it had not grown before.

The driver, Jackson, handled the ribbons Yankee style, fancy, each horse under separate guidance. He was good at it, so good that he could answer questions. A slight

wind was fresh against Buchanan's scarred but comely
face. Old wounds ached a bit from the jouncing, but he
was accustomed to that.

He said, "Down New Mexico the plain's higher by a
couple thousand feet. But this here is greener."

"Water," said Jackson. "Irrigation, some. Whoa there a
bit, Nellie. Gee, Napoleon."

Buchanan thought of the Southwest, where he had
meant to stay awhile, visiting friends. He seemed always to
be going away from home. Right now, it was some kind of
a job offer from Colonel Bradbury, an old acquaintance. It
was coming on evening, and he was to meet the man in
Buffalo, which would be the night stop of the stage.

He thought of Coco Bean, the black prizefighter, who
was somewhere in Montana for a bout. He did not particularly care to catch up to Coco for more than a howdy because of a matter of unsettled business between them. For
some time, the battler had been earnestly seeking to
engage Buchanan in fisticuffs, not out of anger but to decide who was the better man with his fists. And Buchanan
was a peaceable man.

It was not that he feared Coco, who was shorter but
weighed in about the same. It was merely that fighting for
no reason seemed to him to be the most senseless endeav-
or in the world. Also, he was very fond of Coco, and to
hurt him would be an indecent project indeed. He would,
he thought, prepare an alibi, some sort of injury to post-
pone the battle.

That should be easy. Buchanan bore the scars of many
an outraged fortune. On the frontier, the very fact of being
peaceable by nature seemed to invite trouble. People were
always shooting at him or punching at him or cutting holes
in him. It was something he faced with resignation if not
with pleasure.

"Sure is fine cow country,"he said aloud.

"Fine country for killin' people, too," said Jackson.

"That's hard to believe." The evening sky was dark
blue and covered them like a monster bowl. Stars began to
blink behind fantastic, light cloud-banks.

"Nesters," said Jackson. "Little old ranchers scrabblin'

to put a herd together. Bradbury and them call 'em *rustlers*. Whoa there, Dan, easy now, the stable's right nearby."

"Uh, is that *Colonel* Bradbury?"

Jackson turned his weatherbeaten countenance a
quarter way toward Buchanan. "Yep."

"I see." It was a time to keep silence. Buchanan looked
ahead to where, atop a slight grade, a grove of tall trees
shook gently in the breeze. Rustler was a dirty word here,
there, and every place else on the plains of the West. A
man of peace was wise to avoid the subject altogether. He
never knew to whom he might be speaking. The stage
company would be against strife—strife slowed down
movement of people and merchandise. But an employee
could be related to either faction in this kind of controver-
sy. Jackson's side glance might also indicate that he was
suspicious of Buchanan.

That was the way of range wars, neighbor against
neighbor, everyone mistrusting the other. Buchanan was
from East Texas, where his father had been sheriff; he
knew about cattleman against homesteader, big fish
against minnows.

Bradbury was big business, owner of the Bar-B. He had
been one of the first to recognize the advantage of fatten-
ing trail herds on this Wyoming graze, wintering them,
then driving them to railhead for sale. He had prospered
from the start, a bluff and hearty man, loud-voiced, gener-
ous but contentious.

There were others who stood with the colonel from the
start, Dealer Fox of Z-D, a canny veteran; Morgan Crane
of M-C, a violent man. All were middle-aged and set in
their ways, all were vastly wealthy and determined to hold
onto every dollar they did not lavishly spend on themselves and their families.

Buchanan knew these men. He was acquainted with
most of the older frontiersmen, having been up and down
the land for several years, always involved with one cause
or another. They all knew he did not wear a sixgun except
when absolutely necessary. They knew he was a man of
strong convictions, which he kept to himself until occasion

arose. They knew his code, that of the Old West, which held each man accountable to his conscience first and to the law second, which allowed freedom within these boundaries.

He had thought well of Colonel Bradbury. Now he wondered. That word *rustler* rankled in his mind. Too many men had been falsely accused of stealing cattle. Branding of any maverick over a year old and still unmarked was range law. Poor men began by owning a few head, then putting the iron to mavericks. Poor men were most often victims of richer men, Buchanan had noted in his travels. Not that he had anything against the wealthy; most of them had earned their way by hard work and astute management and were to be admired.

Jackson was slowing down the stage as they mounted the gentle rise. Now Buchanan saw his first barbed wire. It ran from the road east to the extent of a section of land, then stretched northward past the grove of trees.

Jackson explained. "Adam Day's farm. That's his wife you seen, the lady passenger."

She was a medium-sized lady in a bonnet and traveling dress. Buchanan had noted her slim ankles. She seemed demure, rather pretty, composed when she had come aboard. The other passengers had been a drummer and two nondescript men of no particular vintage. Buchanan had noted them mechanically, out of habit, without much interest.

Jackson said, "Farmin's good hereabouts. Hard winters make good growin' come spring and summer."

"Vegetables taste better from land like this," Buchanan said. "But what about the bobwire?"

Jackson shook his head. "Cuts across Bar-B graze. Adam and some others took up sections. 'Twarn't Bradbury land, you know. Gov'ment turned it a-loose. But Bradbury was here first. Same old story."

"Man runs a herd long enough, he figures he owns the grass," Buchanan said. "Government's far away, back there in Washington."

"Caused more trouble'n Injun wars," Jackson said. "It'll cause more soon enough."

"You believe that?"

Jackson said, "First off, thought you was one of 'em. Now, seems like you ain't."

"One of what?"

"Those rannies we're carryin'. Hired by the association. Gunners. Bradbury and them are bringin' in an army, like."

"I see." He was uncomfortable. Jackson had guessed right the first time. Bradbury had sent for him. Not for his guns, the colonel knew better than that. For some other reason yet to be divulged—but meaning no good to nesters or small cattlemen, Buchanan knew now.

Jackson said, "Day's house is just beyond the trees, there. I'll be droppin' Miz Day off. Nice people, the Days."

"Most people are, if you get to know 'em."

"Yeah. Well, Adam works hard. Strong-minded man, but honest and all. Crazy about Amanda. That's his wife."

They topped the rise. The view was splendid, the snow-capped, tall mountain ridges plainly visible in the waning light, the sloping land running toward them, birds circling. Big birds, Buchanan noted, black, wide-winged. They were circling.

Jackson said, "Oh, my God and Jesus."

There was a long tree limb outstretched toward the edge of the road. Its burden dangled in awful silence, twisting, turning in the breeze. The man's feet and hands were tied. His head lolled, tongue protruding. It was a bungled job, they had failed to break his neck, he had strangled to death. Buchanan choked on his bile.

Jackson fought the alarmed horses. Buchanan swung down from the high seat and stared upward. There was a sign on the man's chest, crudely lettered.

Rustlers Be Ware.

Jackson was calling, "That's Adam! By damn, it's Adam."

The stage braked to a stop at the side of the road. The passengers piled out. The woman was first, running, screaming, her arms outstretched. The bonnet fell from her head, her hair tumbled down, chestnut color. She was white as a ghost, and now Buchanan saw that she was beautiful in her emotion, star-eyed, weeping. After the first outburst, she was silent. When he caught her, she leaned against him, her face upturned as if she could never stop staring at the body of her husband.

Buchanan said, "Steady. Steady does it."

She was silent, but he felt acquiescence in her. She must be frontier bred, he thought. Now she turned her face away by force of will and looked up at Buchanan. Her lips moved, whispering. He bent to hear her.

"Before God, I'll make them pay. One way or another. They'll pay, damn their souls."

"Yes, ma'am," Buchanan said. "They've got to pay. One way or another."

"Not the law. The law can't touch them."

"There's all kinds of law," he told her. "Some we got to make ourselves."

The two men stood by. The drummer was being sick at the rear wheel of the stage. Jackson held the ribbons in his skillful hands, speechless, agonized.

One of the men said, "Another rustler. Let's git the fool outa here, driver. No business of ours."

Amanda Day pulled loose from Buchanan. She faced the two men. "Rustler? You fools, he was a farmer."

"Prob'ly shot a steer for beef." The man shrugged.

Buchanan said, "Best you get back in the stage. All three of you."

The drummer hastened to obey. The two men faced Buchanan and the lady.

"You tellin' us what to do?"

"Suggestin'," said Buchanan. He spoke to Jackson. "I'll stay with Miz Day. If you run into Coco Bean up in Montana, send him out here. And anybody else might be helpful."

The spokesman said, "One of them, huh?"

"One of them preacher people. Doin' good. Sidin' rustlers."

The woman sprang toward them. "You can't say that about us! You dirty rats . . ."

One of the men reached out to slap her away. The other delved into his pocket for a weapon.

Buchanan left the first man to the woman. He saw her duck and return a blow. The man with the gun was more dangerous. He had cleared it, a small revolver. Buchanan grabbed his wrist and executed a swift turn. The man spun over, head first. The gun dropped to earth. Buchanan kicked it away, then hurled the man into the high wheel of the stage, where he hung, motionless.

Now, the second man was trying to escape Mrs. Day and to yank out a hunting knife, which stuck in its sheath between his shoulder blades. Buchanan took one step and got hold of the man by the nape of the neck. Spinning him, he slammed him alongside the first man. They hung like old clothing for sale, side by side over the rim of the wheel. Mrs. Day was going after them when Buchanan stopped her.

"They didn't hang your husband," he said sharply.

She froze, shoulders slumping. Buchanan went to the pair and one by one he hoisted them into the stagecoach. He took his gear from the boot—rifle, bedroll, carpetbag. He removed his sixgun from its wrappings. He stepped back and fired one shot.

The hanging rope parted. The body of Adam Day slumped to the ground. Mrs. Day let out a little shriek, then stood like a stone, her face a mask.

Buchanan said to Jackson, "Better go ahead. I'll stay and do what's proper."

Jackson looked down at him. "I dunno what your game is. But you better be good at it. Adam was well thought of. This here means trouble in big bunches."

Buchanan sighed. "My game? My game's tryin' to stay out of trouble in big bunches. It just plain never seems to work out. Remember, if you see Coco Bean, the fighter, send him here quick."

"I'll remember." Jackson lowered his voice. "Miz Day, I'm plumb sorrowful. So will they be, your friends."

She nodded. Her glance went to the stiffening body of her husband, then to the horizon, back finally to Buchanan. The stage creaked as the six horses leaned into harness, then rolled toward the town.

Buchanan said, "I can tote him."

"Better we leave him."

Buchanan looked up at the black birds hovering ever nearer. "Buzzards. If you'll go ahead, I'll manage."

She had a small piece of luggage. She hesitated, then said, "It's right kind of you."

It was a strange sight, the woman walking with long strides, Buchanan following with the body over his shoulder. They went past the trees, down the road a hundred yards. They turned off, and the house was another hundred paces from the road. They walked slowly, now. There was a truck garden and fields beyond, where crops were beginning to grow in serrated rows of different hues. There was a barn and a shed. Buchanan went to the shed and found a tarpaulin. He lay the man down and covered him well, tucking in the canvas against rodents. The woman watched him without words.

He said, "Name of Tom Buchanan, ma'am. I'll be fetchin' my soogans. Until somebody comes, I could stick around."

"I'd be grateful, Mr. Buchanan. She spoke as though educated beyond the scope of frontier wives. "I'll be glad of company."

He went to where he had left his gear and brought it to the house. The woman was somewhat chameleonlike, he thought. She had seemed mousy when he first saw her coming aboard the stage. Then, when her emotions were aroused, she had been beautiful as a mama puma in rage. Yet she had quickly regained control of herself.

He entered the house and found it undistinguished, which also was a puzzlement, considering the woman and how she seemed. It needed paint inside and out. It was not as stout-built as needed for Wyoming winters. There was a pump at the sink in the kitchen, which contained a large stove, a table, a half-dozen straight chairs, rude cabinets, a cupboard. Amanda Day had removed her cloak and was coaxing a fire. He waved her away, taking over. She sat down, her face blank.

She wore a blouse and a long traveling skirt. She was younger than he had thought. The lines of her body were long and finely made, her bosom high. Her eyes were hazel, guarded by curved, thick lashes. Her chin was firm but rounded.

There was water in the kettle. The fire leaped, and Buchanan fed it from the wood box. He pumped water and washed himself at the sink, rinsing away the dust of travel, wiping himself dry on his bandanna. The woman watched, and he realized she was coiled, and again he thought of the female puma.

She said, "I must talk. Do you mind if I talk?"

"It's natural," he said. "Better to talk. I'm a good listener."

Her hands twisted in her lap, and he saw that she was not wearing a wedding ring. The fire crackled in the iron stove. She spoke in a low, level tone.

"I left him, you see. That's the trouble. I left him."

"But you were coming back?"

"Yes. I pawned the ring to pay the fare. I thought of him, lonely, caring, worrying. I was the schoolteacher. He was the farmer from Indiana. For three years I tried. Then I failed him. The winters, the loneliness. I am from San Francisco. Do you know what I mean?"

"Reckon I do."

"The work. So hard. The chores. He hired when he needed help, the most of it he wanted to do himself. He was very strong. At night, he would be asleep over his supper. In the morning, he was a giant for the work. It was too much."

"Gets that way, sometimes." He recognized what she was telling him. He knew how women suffered on the frontier when their men worked too hard, stayed away too long, were not easy and smiling and comfortable in the bed. It was one of the reasons he had shied away from marriage.

"At first we had . . . love. He was handsome. You'd never know, looking at that . . . him . . . that . . ." She bit her lip, a shudder running the length of her body and limbs. She shook her head. "Love doesn't thrive on a one-man farm. It flies out the window on a summer breeze. Loneliness takes over. But I cared for him . . . about him. Until we quarreled."

Buchanan filled in the pause. "My Pa used to say, 'Love in a tub—and the bottom fell out.' Can be fixed sometimes."

"Sometimes . . . I saw the war coming. I knew we were in the way. Our wire was cut so often, our crops trampled. It's not going to get better."

"Things generally get worse before they get better."

"Colonel Bradbury offered to buy us out. It wasn't much money, but it would have provided a new start, in different country. Adam wouldn't have it. He had learned to love this country. He had worked since he was eighteen to have a place of his own. It was his religion."

"Man's like that." And poor Adam Day had died on his land in the most terrible fashion.

"So I left him."

"Reckon you didn't want to leave."

"I didn't want to leave him. But I'd learned to hate this place. I'd learned to hate farming. It was a mistake from the start." She drew herself up. "Which does not mean that I accept Adam's murder."

"No. I can see that."

"I'll sell to Bradbury. And I'll use the money to bring in law, for the little ranchers and farmers." Her eyes blazed.

Buchanan shook his head. "They already bought the law. It's the way they do. Seen it before. Time'll come. But it ain't here yet."

"I'll go to Washington."

"Seen that, too. By the time anything happens, the war's over, and everybody left alive is plumb peaceable and agreeable."

"Something must be done. I won't quit until it happens."

"Yes, ma'am." She was heading for another disaster. Maybe she was that kind, doomed to losing. He replenished the blazing fire. The kettle was beginning to heat up. He looked in a cupboard and found coffee and a grinder.

He turned the handle, and the aroma of the bean came into the room, soothing, promising.

"You don't think anything can be done."

"Not thataway, ma'am. I'd let it rest, think on it."

"You're like the rest of them," she flared at him. "Afraid to make a move. Afraid nothing will come of it. Afraid to take a chance."

"Well, now, I'm kind of a peaceable fella," he told her. "I am against lynchin'. Feel pretty strong about it. Wouldn't say I'm goin' to duck out, run away. But it's best to bide time until the cards are on the table."

"Just like Adam. Bide your time, bide your time." She stood, her hands doubled into fists. "Men! Damn all men in this country."

She ran out of the kitchen. Buchanan tended the fire. The water would boil in a few moments. He had not eaten since noon, and now night was coming on. His huge frame demanded food. He found a pan and some bacon grease and eggs and bread gone stale. He put on the pan and opened the stove and toasted the bread on a long fork. He put the toast on the warming shelf and found two platters and made the coffee and broke eggs into the pan.

She came back into the kitchen. She was wearing Levis and boots and a wool shirt. Her hair was braided and wound around her head. She was handsome and strong again and able to smile ruefully.

"I have a temper, you see. I apologize. You've been more than kind."

"Think nothin' of it, ma'am. Set yourself and eat. No matter what, a body's got to eat."

It was amazing what strong coffee and simple food could do—but she was an unusual woman, Buchanan was learning. Now she wanted to listen, and he talked about himself a little, telling her of his roving life and of his trials and tribulations in seeking peace, making it comical and light so that she smiled, almost laughed, caught herself and sobered.

"Coco, you mentioned a Coco Bean?"

"A black man, a prizefighter. A friend." He told her of

Coco's consuming desire to match himself at fisticuffs against Buchanan. He told her of Coco's fear of firearms, with which he was continually becoming involved. "Me and Coco. Always in trouble, one ruckus after another."

She said, "I read in the paper before I left about a prizefight. In Butte, I believe."

"Nobody beats Coco," said Buchanan. "Right now I wish he was here. He's a comfortin' man to have beside you."

"You're a comforting man yourself, Buchanan."

"Well, thankee." He hesitated, then went on. "You say Colonel Bradbury offered to buy you out?"

"He did. I don't think he's an evil man."

"He sent for me. Now you see, he knows I'm not violent, like. Maybe he thought things could be straightened out with some doin' of mine. No guns."

"I wouldn't deny it. Morgan Crane is different, headstrong, an angry man. Dealer Fox is properly named, devious, not to be trusted. The others sway with the winds. Bradbury's foreman is Sime Pollard, said to be a killer."

"Sime Pollard. Yes, indeed." Pollard was a fine cattleman, but he was a quick gun when provoked. Buchanan had known and disliked Pollard years before, in the Southwest.

"Then there's Jigger Dorn. He's new, they brought him in. It's said Dorn will call in other gunmen."

"Yes. Dorn will get them if somebody wants them. That's his business. Calls himself a lawman. He'll wear anybody's badge for a price."

"The town is under control of the big people, of course."

"Town's got to make do with money from ranchers and farmers."

She said, "The other people, Adam's friends . . ." She broke off as a wagon rattled outside and jangled to a stop.

Buchanan picked up his sixgun from where he had placed it conveniently on a shelf. They went to the door. She held a lamp, and Buchanan stayed out of the light. A man and a woman called out and came toward the house.

"It's the Kovacses," said Mrs. Day. "And the girl, Raven. They're our people."

The man was short of stature and thick-bodied, round-headed, bearded, blue-eyed. His wife was the same height and could have been his sister, sturdy, thick-limbed, pleasant of mien. The girl was slim and dark with black hair down to her waist. She was, Buchanan realized, an Indian.

They murmured their condolences, and Mrs. Day wept in reaction. Buchanan took the man—his name was Pieter Kovacs—to the shed. They uncovered the body, the message still pinned to the hickory shirt.

"A lie," said Kovacs.

"Best look in the barn." They found a lantern and Kovacs held it high in the dimness. Chickens squawked and ran underfoot. A work horse neighed and Buchanan found the oat bin and fed him. An old dog raised his head, blinked, and went back to sleep.

Buchanan looked around. There was a fresh hide flung across a sawhorse. Fresh beef hung in hooks along a wall. The brand on the hide was Bar-B.

Harness was tossed in a jangled heap. Buchanan picked it up, looked at the hook where the carcass was hung. He snorted.

"A lousy frame-up."

"Is so."

"Somebody killed the beef and hung it on the harness hooks. No farmer would do that, harness is precious and hard to come by."

"By me this is true."

"They must've been real mad at him."

"Ah, yes. While the missus was away." Kovacs spoke with an accent, but his meaning was clear. "Adam, he was upset, no? He went to town. Bradbury offer to buy him out. Adam cursed. Because of the missus, you see?"

"Sure. I see."

"Adam cursed Bradbury. Pollard, he got in the way. Adam, he hit Pollard."

"He hit Pollard and lived?"

"In town, it was. Adam he never carried gun. This is known. Pollard, he made threats."

"Kept his promise, seems like."

"Yes. Everyone will know. And nothing will be done."
Kovacs was bitter. "I too have been asked to sell to the
Cattleman's Association. And others."

"You thinkin' on it?"

The man's blue eyes became flinty in the light of the
lantern. "Not thinking. Not selling."

"You know what it means?"

"I know." He gestured. "I am from Poland. I know
trouble, bad trouble."

Buchanan said, "Maybe you do. But I got a notion that
this means a range war. And until you get into one of
them rangdoodles . . . you're just an amateur of trouble."

"They cannot hang us all." He hesitated. "Something
should be done about Adam, no?"

Buchanan debated a moment. He was into it now
whether or not he liked it. A lynching was a horror to him.
He said slowly, "You got a wagon. It won't be safe around
here from now on. Maybe we better take Adam to town."

"To town?" Kovacs brightened. "Ah. Is so."

Buchanan went for his guns and his belongings. Once
again, it had happened to him. Fate was against a man of
peace, he recognized. Fate . . . and people.

2

Buffalo was a small town trying to find its place in the rich land all about. Its Main Street was wide but not very long. There was the general store, the smithy, the one-storied hotel and way station for the stage, two saloons, and scattered dwellings for the people of the community. There was no local law, only the sheriff based in Sheridan who came that way so seldom as to be a stranger.

In back of the Powder River Saloon, there was a large room for the cattlemen's pleasure. Pat Noonan, who owned the place, was a Celtic gentleman with an eye to profit and a throat for whiskey. The back room was kept sacred to the nabobs of cattledom, Sheridan County style. A quota was then present, bottles on the tables, glasses clinking. The mood, however, was somber.

Outside, horses wearing the Bar-B, the Z-D, the M-C, and other brands lined the hitching racks on both sides of the street. Men entered and left the other barroom, the Deuces Wild, gathered in small knots talking. They were lean men, riders, clanking their spurs. They were restless this night.

In the rear of the Powder River, Colonel Bradbury brooded. He was a florid man, bulky, big-nosed, full-lipped. He wore a mustache and a trimmed beard. He affected soft buckskins and leggings and wore a hat with slanting brim.

Sime Pollard, the colonel's foreman, leaned against the wall, his lips tight. There was a slight bruise along his jaw-line. He was a big man with long arms dangling to his knees, and he now wore two sixguns tied low on his thighs.

Bradbury said, "I don't like it a damn bit."

A blond man in tweeds and a hunter's cap said, "Rotten bad, you know. Against it, always have been."

"We're all against it, Trevor," Bradbury said heavily. "Still, it had to come. Adam was stubborn. They're all stubborn."

"Have a right, haven't they?" The Englishman had gray eyes and smooth skin.

Dealer Fox said, "You two, I declare." His eyes were close set, his mouth turned down, a thin man always thinking in devious fashion.

Morgan Crane was a giant. He wore his round hat square on his head, his jaw thrust forward, his irregular teeth showed but not in a grin. "Day had it comin', I tell you. Got to clear 'em all out. No other way. We cut their fence, they mend it. Cows hung on it half the time. How we ever gonna grow with them chokin' off the graze?"

"Matter of human rights," Trevor said. His voice was light, he seemed frail compared to the others. "Man's home his castle, all that y' know."

"Damn their lousy cabins," Crane roared. "Castles my left hind foot."

"Caught him redhanded, slicin' up your beef," said Fox.

Trevor said, "I rather doubt that."

Pollard moved against the wall, his hand going to his gun butt. "Don't call me no liar."

Trevor ignored him. "Should turn the fella over to the law, say I."

Bradbury said, "Whoa, now. Pollard caught him. One of your riders was along."

"Oh, yes. And one of Mr. Fox's men and one from M-C. Rather odd, what? I mean, they ridin' together and goin' straight to Day's place and all that rot?"

"He's callin' us all liars," said Pollard. "We tracked him down, is the way it was."

"And strung him up without a trial."

"He got a trial. Judge Lynch presidin'," said Dealer Fox. "My man told me."

"Ain't you never heard of loyalty to your men?" demanded Crane. "Didn't they teach you nothin' in bloody old England?"

Trevor did not lose his calm manner. "They taught me to honor the law of the land."

"Judge Lynch is the law of this damn land."

"It is a very bad law," said Trevor. "The common law of this country is based on Blackstone. A man is innocent until he is proven guilty by a jury of his peers."

"That law's too damn common." Crane laughed loudly at his own remark. "Peers. I hear you're a damn peer. Have we got to get a bunch of galoots like you to hold a trial?"

Trevor said, "I've always thought you were uncouth, Crane. Now it is proven. Colonel Bradbury, if no action is taken against your man, Pollard, I'm afraid I must take steps."

"Now, Trevor. You got to understand. These people have moved in on us. We were here first. They will undermine us if we let 'em. Why, you've lost cattle your own self. You know they're rustlin' a herd here and there, sellin' it off in Montana or Colorado."

"Not proven against Adam Day, a farmer."

"Stealin' one head's as bad as rustlin' a hundred."

"You believe that?"

"It ain't like he needed it for food. Nobody minds if a man's hungry, he butchers a steer now and then. Day's a troublemaker."

"Was. Was a man," said Trevor.

"Wait a minute," Crane shouted. "He said 'steps.' I wanta know what he means by that."

"Yes, Trevor. What steps?" asked Dealer Fox.

Pollard moved again. Bradbury stared at him, scowled, shook his head.

Trevor said, "If you persist in ignoring the law, I must turn in my resignation as a member of the Cattleman's Association."

"That means you're goin' agin us."

"That means I will not associate in your actions."

"Then you're agin us," said Crane. "Why, your own men'll quit. They won't fight us."

"Just a minute," Bradbury said. "Trevor, here, he's been here a long time. Invested a lot of his money, built himself a fine spread. He's entitled to his say. He can't help but be one of us. He's big business hereabouts."

"He'll be small potatoes if he pulls out," said Crane. "This here's war. A man's either with us or agin us."

"War," said Trevor softly. "Jigger Dorn. Men like him. Like Pollard. Against a few grangers and small ranchers. Unequal, what?"

Bradbury said, "It's better for them this way, don't you see? Set a few examples, show force they know they can't whip. Kovacs, now, you know how he is. Mule-headed. Rob Whelan, him and his ex-whore wife, he's another. Cut them people down and the rest of 'em will quit, leave the country."

"One merely kills a few, eh? Human sacrifices, as in the Bible?" Trevor shook his head sadly. "Not cricket, old man, not at all cricket."

"Bugs ain't got nothin' to do with it," Crane roared. "Crickets be damn. We got to either stop the rustlin' now or lose everything we got with our hard work."

"I suggest the rustling is being done by a gang taking advantage of the situation," said Trevor. "Trailed a herd myself last month. Nobody from here involved. Four or five men driving over the mountains, through the pass into Montana. Not our people at all."

"You couldn't track a cat in your own yard," said Crane. "I believe you are agin us. I never did like your palaver. My gran'daddy fit you people at N'Yorleans and whupped you. Come over here with your money and buy your way in, then lord it over everybody."

Trevor said, "I repeat, Crane, you are a boor. I might add that never did I care for your loud mouth."

The big man knocked over his chair as he leaped to his feet. "By God, I don't take that from any man."

Bradbury said, "Here now. None of that. You asked for it, Morgan. You've been askin' for it. Just simmer down."

"I'll clean him good," raved Crane. "I'll mow him down and tromp on him."

"No," said Bradbury.

Trevor smiled faintly. "He's such a windbag. Why not let him try it?"

Bradbury said, "He's too big for you, Trevor. You ought to know that."

"Not at all," said the Englishman. "I'd be happy to oblige him. He's a clumsy clown, you know. Isn't he, now?"

Crane lunged. Trevor stepped aside, then back in. His left fist shot out. It clipped Crane in the eye. The big man roared again but could not stop his forward impetus. He ran into the wall when Pollard moved away.

Bradbury said, "I said no. I mean no."

"You can't stop me!" Crane was coming around.

The door to the saloon banged open. Pat Noonan stuck in his head and called, "You gents better come on out here. There's somethin' goin' on you ain't gonna like."

"What? What is it, Noonan?"

"Might say it's a parade. Only it's bein' led by a corpus. Better come and see for yourselfs."

Crane started to yell, was stopped by Bradbury's quick gesture. He mumbled something about killing Trevor and was escorted out of the room by Pollard and Fox.

Bradbury said, "I think you're making a bad enemy, Trevor."

"Oh, quite. Always detested the man. Should we join the gawkers?"

"Crane can be real mean," warned Bradbury. "I can only hold him back a wee bit when he gets started."

"You needn't hold him back, old man."

They went through the bar, which was deserted. Bradbury insisted, "You know what Abe Lincoln said. 'We got to hang together or we'll hang separate.' "

"Benjamin Franklin," murmured Trevor. " 'We must all hang together or assuredly we shall all hang separately.' Upon the signing of your Declaration of Independence. Not quite apt under these circumstances, what?"

But Bradbury was staring at the street, where pine torches gave more light than had ever shone on a moonless night in Buffalo. People lined up on the boardwalk across from the saloon. None were of the Cattleman's Association, most were faceless people beneath the notice of the mighty.

A wagon was coming slowly toward them. Two riders, a man and a woman, rode beside it. Behind it, a man in a fur hat rode a tall mule. Three people were on the wide seat of the wagon, sitting straight.

The driver was Pieter Kovacs. His wife was at his side. Next to her was Amanda Day.

In the wagon body stood Tom Buchanan, legs spread apart. With his knees, he supported a reclining board, set at an angle that allowed all to see its burden. Buchanan held a newly lit torch, which burned fierce and bright.

The light of the torch fell upon the contorted face of Adam Day as he lay bound to the plank.

Trevor said, "Damn. Now it's down the drain."

Bradbury could only stare. His stomach turned over. He tried to look away and could not. He knew Trevor was correct, the challenge was there, plain to see and understand.

Sime Pollard was ghastly in the flickering light. He moved close to his boss, and another man, all in black, came to stand beside him. This man smiled at the sight of the procession. His name was Jigger Dorn, and he smiled often and laughed a lot, even while cutting down another victim with his swift guns.

Pollard said hoarsely, "Let us get 'em now, Boss."

Bradbury found his voice. "That's . . . that's Tom Buchanan in the wagon. Buchanan! I sent for him to work for us!"

"Wrong man," said Trevor.

"Damn it, I hoped he could keep the peace. Buchanan never wants to get into a fight."

"Perhaps not," said Trevor. "But there he is."

"Let us get them," Pollard said again. "Me and Jigger."

"And have the whole damn town on us?" Bradbury fought for control. "You want to wipe out the town?"

"Now or some other time," said Pollard. "I know the feelin' around. They ain't for us."

Dealer Fox said, "Pollard's right. But we can't do it. The governor'd be in with the army."

"We own the damn gov'nor," said Morgan Crane.

"Not to that extent," Trevor warned them.

"No," said Bradbury heavily. "We got to let this ride. We got to make plans. You'll get your chance, Sime, you and Dorn and the rest of you. It's got to come. I see it now. I thought maybe . . . but there's Buchanan ridin' with 'em."

"Judge Lynch," said Trevor. "Very great man, you said. Nothing like setting an example. Well, gentlemen. I bid you farewell."

He brushed between Pollard and Dorn. He ran lightly, a slim figure, to the side of the wagon. The horseman and the man on the mule drew in. Trevor smiled and put up a hand to Buchanan, who peered down at him.

"What the hell?" Dealer Fox said.

"He . . . he told us goodbye."

"Let me gun him," begged Pollard.

Buchanan now took Trevor's hand and lifted him into the wagon. A murmur ran along the line of citizens watching with their torches beginning to burn low.

Morgan Crane bellowed, "A goddam Benedict Arnold. I told you. Them damn Britishers ain't to be trusted nohow, no time, nowhere."

Two more men pulled in alongside Pollard and Dorn. They were squat, ugly Toad Tanner and ancient, evil Dab Geer. All looked at Bradbury. "That Buchanan stove up Cactus an' Dorgan."

"No," he said. "The country won't stand for no massacree in the streets of the town. This has got to be done smartlike."

"Yep," said Dealer Fox. His eyes were gleaming. "Come inside. Pay them no heed."

Bradbury turned. Crane reluctantly followed, then Pollard. The hired gunmen remained in front of the saloon, watching, hands fluttering near their gun butts. Their eyes followed Trevor, now standing with Buchanan, helping to keep the pitiful corpse from rolling as the wagon slid in the ruts of the dirt street.

In the back room of the Powder River Saloon, Dealer Fox said, "Sime, you mind that door."

"I hope you got somethin' good," said Crane. "I hope to hell it has to do with that British bastard."

"You got your hope," said Fox.

"Like how?"

"You see he's left us, joined them. You know how he is, thickheaded. Okay. His house is built of wood. His barn's full of hay. Supposin' it got burned down right quick?"

"No," said Bradbury. "He's got friends a-plenty."

"Supposin' we make it like the nesters done it, startin' a war because of Adam Day?"

Crane said, "Hey, that's mighty good. Leave somethin' around like it was them. Pollard and his boys can do it."

"It's for the good of us all," said Fox. It's for the country in the long run. We all agreed on that."

"I don't like it," said Bradbury. But he was in it. He visualized his holdings in distress, his herd scattered—even the burning of his own house. It had to be nipped in the bud. It had to be stopped before he was cut off from all his ambitious aims, politics, Washington.

"It's a hiyu notion," said Crane.

"It can work. We'll never be caught at it," said Fox.

"For the benefit of all," Bradbury murmured.

"You betcha," said Crane. "How 'bout it, Sime? And turn loose his cavvy and take a run at his herd, scatter it. Anybody tries to stop you, kill 'em and leave 'em where they'll get the blame, see?"

"Best if it works that way," said Fox.

"Boss?" Pollard looked at Bradbury and received a nod. "Okay. And believe me, Trevor's men won't do nothin'. We talked to 'em. They don't cotton to his ways. Like cleanin' outhouses alla time. Baths, he wants 'em to bathe durin' the week, even. And the way he talks through his nose and all. They won't make a move. We'll tell 'em to run off, leave the country."

Bradbury took out a roll of currency. "Pay them off. Makes for good feelin' thataway."

"Pay 'em nothin'," said Crane. "Not me, I won't."

Fox added some money. "Brad's right. Smooth things over best we can."

"People around here's got to learn which side their bread's buttered on," said Crane.

"For their own good," Bradbury felt compelled to say. He had to make himself believe it. He tried very hard to believe it.

3

The grave was deep. They wrapped Adam Day in a blanket and lowered him and stood irresolute with the shovels. The old man took off his fur cap and came forward.

"You all know me. Dan Badger. I come into the mountains in '35, a youngun, green as buff'lo grass. Me and the others, we walked the ranges and down into Yellowstone and up to Canady and down to Mexico. We seen it all. We seen you folks come in and it was good. And we seen the cattle fatten and it was good. And now, because of the good things, we come to bad things. And this yere is one of 'em, this lynchin' of a good man, Adam Day. And I say to the Lord, an eye for an eye, a tooth for a tooth, like it was laid down. And I say Adam was the first man, and now this yere Adam is first to be martyred in this yere country. And it's a bad thing, Lord, but we must face up to it. I never fit Indians, Lord, because they was friendlies. And they had to go, and I'm plumb sad about that. But this kinda thing, Lord, this has got to stop so our mountains and our plains and our valleys shan't suffer under the cloud of Your wrath . . . Amen."

Half the town was there, not many people, the storekeeper and the blacksmith and some others. A chorus of murmured *amens* fell softly on the night. Buchanan and Kovacs began to shovel dirt into the grave.

The woman was tearless. She stood with Mrs. Kovacs and the couple who had ridden with them, the Whelans, a young man with a face too old and a young woman, pretty but with eyes that could grow hard and cold. They owned a small ranch, they had lived a lot in other places, and they knew what had to come. Raven Kovacs rode a buckskin pony from which she did not dismount. Jack Trevor held his hat over his heart and was silent.

The sound of clods falling on the dead man was forlorn. Some of the townsfolk turned away, the others followed until there was the small knot of them who were aware of what was portended. Buchanan knew who they were by now. He plied the long-handled shovel, and his mind went around, and he knew that once again he was in for it.

When the task was finished he said to Trevor. "You know where Bradbury might be?"

"I do."

"Will you take me to him?"

"A pleasure," said Trevor.

"There's gunnies around," Rob Whelan warned. "We better cover you."

The wife, Fay Whelan, wore a gunbelt and a holster as though they belonged upon her.

Buchanan said gently, "Why, now, it's against my habit, but I happen to be carryin' a Colt tonight. Don't put yourselves in no trouble for me."

"Nor I," said Trevor. "They won't make a move in town this night."

"We must make plans," said Kovacs. "They will move when they have time to think."

"Better go on home," Buchanan said. "I'll come to you when I can learn a thing or two."

Kovacs said, "Yes. Best to go home now. Meet tomorrow at my place?"

"There's gonna be a war," said Whelan. "I been in range wars. I'm warnin' yawl."

The old mountain man said, "I knew Adam Day. He was good to me. I will ride here and there. Then I will let you know."

"That is good," said Kovacs. "Nobody knows where Dan Badger rides."

Buchanan said, "Yeah. Well, drop my gear at the hotel. I'll be seein' you."

Amanda Day came to him. "I'll go with the Kovacs tonight. But I want to thank you, Buchanan. I want you to know I believe in you."

"Just don't fret too much," he said. "It's a hard way to live, but don't fret too much."

He watched them go. The Indian girl rode the pony as though born in the saddle. The wagon rumbled, the Whelans, always side by side, went into the night. Trevor inhaled.

"A man makes a choice, eh? Must do. It's a bad situation, Buchanan."

"Whelan. He looks familiar," said Buchanan.

"It is told that he was once a hired gun. The lady, well . . . a dance hall girl. They married and came up here and homesteaded. But they are cattle people, so their stock is vulnerable, on open range, y' see?"

"I see it too well," said Buchanan. "Let's talk to the colonel and them."

They walked to town. Trevor was incisive and clear in his recitation. He laid out the scene from the point of view of the ranchers.

"There are rustlers. We've all lost beef. But Adam Day was no rustler. His mistake was in mauling Pollard. You know, one of my own men was along when they did it. I've long suspected my employees are not to be trusted."

"Then you're in real trouble, Trevor."

"Oh, yes."

"You stand to lose a lot."

"Quite."

"They didn't let you in on the plot against Day?"

"Of course not. I believe that was Pollard's revenge. I believe Crane and Fox wanted to begin a war, and this was the way Pollard chose."

"You tote a gun, Trevor?"

"Beneath this jacket. Snug, you see?"

"If you can get it out."

Trevor made a lightning pass. A short-barreled Smith & Wesson .38 appeared in his hand. "Gambler fella was in town. Broke. Staked him, fed him a bit at the ranch. Tried to teach me the regular way, no good at all. This came easy."

"Gambler name of Luke Post?"

"Why, right-o. You know him?"

"I know him.

"Fine chap. Taught me a lot."

"He taught you right good." They had come to the edge of the tiny settlement. "Funny, these here people make their livin' mostly off the big ranchers. But when the Indian gal rode in and told 'em what was up, they all come out with their torches."

"Very British, therefore very American," said Trevor. "Your heritage lies in our nation, y' know."

"My grandma was born in Scotland. No love for your people. But I see what you mean."

People still talked in little shoals. They walked to the Powder River Saloon, and Trevor looked up and down the racks and said, "Odd. Pollard and the men are gone. But Bradbury's horse is here. And, yes, Crane's and Fox's."

"Trouble, trouble," said Buchanan. "Let's have a palaver with the big men."

Noonan eyed them with suspicion and a bit of fear as

they went to the back room. Buchanan slammed open the door, and Trevor followed him in. The men at the table started back, Crane kicked over his chair.

Buchanan said, "Well, Colonel, here I am."

"You . . . you hired out to me, and then you crossed me."

Crane said, "And look, he already picked up with that goddam British bastard."

Fox edged his chair away from the table. "What do you want? You get nothin' from us. You showed your colors, the both of you."

"Raisin' the good town people agin us," said Bradbury. "You caused a lot of harm here tonight, Buchanan."

"With some help from me, I hope," said Trevor.

"You double crossin' sonofabitch." Crane came in a rush. "I'll take you apart."

Trevor's gun slid out. Buchanan stepped in front of him. Trevor covered the other two.

Buchanan met Crane, took hold of him with his left hand, and stopped the giant in his tracks. He said, "You sure use a lot of bad language, Crane. I know you're Crane because I been warned against that bad tongue of yours."

Crane tried to kick to the groin. Buchanan shook him once, then shoved him against the wall, so that he bounced like a rubber ball. As he rebounded, Buchanan hit him with a right hand. Crane went off his feet, staggered, sighed. Then he dropped to the floor in a heap.

Trevor said, "Now that was neat. That was quite the old neat bit. I do like that."

Buchanan addressed Bradbury. "I never signed on with you. I came up here to look around and maybe do what I could. But you never told me what was doin'. You never told me you were out to hang farmers."

"A rustler. Day was a rustler."

"You're a liar. I saw the hide, I saw the way it was planted. I saw enough to know it was a frame-up."

Fox squealed, "You better be careful who you accuse."

"Accuse? Why, mister, when I accuse someone, it'll be to his face. And he's likely to stand trial. Because I'll have proof that he's guilty. I'm tellin' you Adam Day was framed and lynched. You can take it from there."

Bradbury said, "You better not butt into this, Buchanan. I'll pay your fare back to New Mexico. You better take the stage south."

Fox said, "When Morgan gets his gun, you better make yourself scarce. We got men can take care of people like you. And you, too, Trevor."

"They do run off at the mouth, now, don't they?" Buchanan asked of Trevor.

"Very often."

"You'll see," said Fox. "You'll see soon enough."

Bradbury said, "Shut up, Dealer. There's been too much talk, like Buchanan says. I didn't want it this way. But now it's come to pass, we'll do what we got to do. You better get out. This here is war."

"Uh-huh," said Buchanan. "And you used to be a right decent *hombre*. I mind when you was as good a man as need be. Didn't have much then. Yep, you wasn't a bad sort. Well, be seein' you."

He turned his back. Trevor's eyes were on Dealer Fox, on Crane struggling to regain his senses.

At the door, Trevor said, "Quite right. We'll be seeing you chaps. Buchanan has agreed to work for me. Toodle-oo, men."

They went out through the saloon, now nearly empty. Trevor led the way to the hotel. A wizened man with one arm greeted them warmly. His name was Weevil, and he had been a wrangler until his accident.

"Took guts to do what you folks did tonight. People's with you. But don't count on 'em. They just pore folks. They're no fighters."

"Thank you for the kind words," said Trevor. "Put us in adjoining rooms, please."

"Already got Mr. Buchanan fixed up in number nine. You can have number eight for the night, then. I'll have your hoss tended to." He reached beneath the counter. "Got a bottle of Monongahela here. Thought you might want a nightcap. Got some cold venison and cheese, too."

"Excellent notion," said Trevor. "Put it on my bill."

They went back down a narrow hall and to their rooms. Neither was ready for sleep. Weevil brought them the cold food, and they sat in Buchanan's room and ate and talked and sipped at the whiskey.

Amanda Day slumped wearily in the wagon. It had been a long ride out to the Kovacs' place, but she could not have returned home this night. She could not help remembering Adam's face, the protruding tongue, the wry neck where the rope had bitten. They had been quarreling, she had found she did not truly love him, but the sight of him burned into her memory, and she knew she would never be rid of it.

She had visited the Kovacs' house only once and knew little about it except that it resembled a blockhouse. It had been a fort, a small rallying ground of the mountain men, built of native stone against Indian raids. Kovacs had rebuilt it, adding the kitchen on the back, still using stone hauled by his workhorses, patiently putting it together with skills he had brought from the Old World. It could be depressing viewed from without, but inside, Jenny had made it comfortable. It was cool in summertime and easy to heat in the winters. For now, it was a resting place.

Kovacs put the horses in the stone barn. Raven worked with him, quick, efficient, smiling, looking often at Dan Badger as he watered and fed the tall mule.

Badger said, "Man alone in these parts, he sees things. Them cattlemen, they're bringin' in gunmen. They'll be up to deviltry."

"Is so," replied Kovacs.

"This man Buchanan. Hang onto him if you kin."

"Not his fight."

"I seen his kind. He cut Adam down, he rode with you all in the wagon. Count on him."

"Maybe so."

"This is a good place to make a fight. Put in grub. Don't go anywheres alone. Watch the womenfolk. Lemme do the scoutin'. Nobody knows the country like us mountainy men."

"Is so."

Badger looked long at Raven. "You know what to do."

"Yes, Dan Badger." She had been rescued from a battlefield and nursed back to health by the Kovacs, and the mountain man had never been far away when he might be needed.

Badger mounted the mule and rode out. Kovacs and Raven finished the chores together, then went into the house.

Amanda Day was moving about as in a dream, frowning. Kovacs touched her arm and led her into the huge front room of the house. The hall was baronial in height, the furniture heavy polished oak. Large bedrooms were off to either side. Between the kitchen and the big room, there was a hall and two closets. It was a most unusual house for this clime and time. There was a big fireplace built into one wall. The windows were narrow, but Kovacs had found glass for them.

She said, "You have built a castle, Pieter."

"I talk to Adam." He ignored her compliment.

"Yes. He trusted you."

"You talk to me."

"I was coming back to him. But something had gone, Pieter. His mind was narrow, like those windows. He had grown hard."

"Hard country."

"For a farmer, yes. You have cattle and vegetables and wheat. You have built well."

"No good now, mebbe."

"You're right. I saw it coming. I told Adam. He hated me for telling."

"Because truth."

"Maybe. He drove me away. I couldn't stay away. It was like quitting. But I didn't want to come back. I had to. But I didn't want to."

"Is so." He lit a briar pipe and waited.

She said, "The man, Buchanan. Is that what you want to know about?"

He nodded, puffing.

"He'll help. He's not with them."

"You sure?"

"Positive." She was surprised at her own emphasis. "He came to take a job with Bradbury, but when he saw . . . saw Adam . . . he whipped two men for calling us rustlers."

"Badger?"

"Why, you know Dan. Homeless, aimless now. But a good man."

"Whelan?"

"They had nothing. They are trying to make something for themselves. I wouldn't wonder they'd be the next target, living out there, grazing on government land."

"Is so." He sighed. "You and me, we know, now. It will be very bad."

"Yes, it will be terrible."

"We must fight."

"I agree."

"You could go."

"I won't go." She drew a breath. "I see. You mean that I did not love Adam in the end. That it was over between us. You think I have no stake?"

"Is so."

"They hanged him," she said. "I saw him. If he were a stranger, I would hate them, want them to be punished."

He nodded. "Then we know. Buchanan, he can be of big help. Tomorrow we will know. So quick." He looked around at his comfortable house. "In Poland it was pogroms. Here it is the same. The world is made right, no? But people. There is something wrong with people."

"Not all people," she insisted. "I won't believe that."

"Mebbeso." He closed his eyes.

She thought of Buchanaan and how he had been so quickly brutal against the two gunmen and so kind when they were alone. More men like Buchanan, she prayed, spare these good folk, spare them please God.

The F-Bar ranch was small, it was in the open country of the high plain. The Whelans ran only a couple of hundred head, but in the couple of years they had been in Wyoming, that small herd had been bred up to sturdiness and solid flesh. Their house was small but tight, sparsely furnished. They had lived low on the hog since departing the Texas border.

They sat on the top rail of the corral in the night. All was quiet and peaceful, there were trees nearby, a creek ran close to the homestead. They sat close together without actually touching elbows.

He bore scars, he had been a gunner in his day. Scarcely thirty, he had lived three lifetimes, a part of which had been behind bars. He knew many things he did not need to know and a few things he did. He had been a kid on the trails, and he had been a faro dealer in gambling halls. His nose was dented and slightly awry, his eyes deep-set, his skin rough with the outdoor labors that had occupied him since he and Fay had finally shaken loose from the past.

Fay Delehanty's real name was something now hazy in her mind. She had been born in Kansas City to a mother who had, to say the least, been careless. Her father could have been any one of many, none worth remembering. Her childhood had been spent in various houses of prostitution between Kansas and Texas.

Somehow a spark had kindled in the girl, somehow she wanted that which she did not have. It was no great ambition, looking at frontier wives, but it was in her and it remained her goal through thick and thin, mostly thin. She longed for a small spread, a house which was a home, and a man with the guts to make it all come true.

It had all come together in El Paso. She was working in the Ace-Deuce Saloon. Rob, two years out of the penitentiary, had scrabbled together a few head of cattle, had come to look for a drink and a woman before heading northward where he was unknown, where the grass was high, where he could get the fresh start, which was the holy privilege of everyone on the western frontier.

They looked at each other. She was red-haired, rouged, attired in a tawdry short skirt. He was saddleworn and scarred. Each liked what was there, inside the other person. Each had been around long enough to look beneath the surface of a person.

There was a gambler, Cat Bundy, who had long been

trying to get Fay to work for him, bragging about his con-
nections with the elite, promising her a house of her own.
When he saw them together, heads close, murmuring, he
took umbrage. He grabbed Rob and yanked him away
from the girl.

Rob knew his lesson in this situation: take it easy, give
the other man first shot, do anything to stay inside the law.
He allowed himself to be pushed against the bar. He allowed himself to be upbraided for stealing another man's
woman. His hand did not go near his Colt.

Marshal Spencer came into the Ace-Deuce. He listened.
Fay ran to him, knowing him for a decent human being.
He went to Cat Bundy, who was of the opposite political
faction, and turned him away from Rob.

Bundy went for his hidey gun. Rob hit him once with
his fist and once with the muzzle of the long-barreled .45,
which he produced with lightning speed.

Bundy fell down and died of a fractured skull. Marshal
Spencer helped Fay pack her few belongings. In a few
hours, the couple were married by a preacher known to
the marshal and on their way to camp and the little herd
and eventually Wyoming. And now they sat on the rail
and wondered.

She said, "So quietlike."

"Huh-huh. Good country."

"Best country I ever seen," she said. "Almost made it
here, didn't we?"

"Almost."

"People. The land's beautiful. The people are manure."

"You shouldn't speak like o' that, Fay," he said. "We
promised not to talk like o' that no more."

"Sure, we did. And kept our promise. Now . . . what the
hell's the use?"

"We ain't dead yet."

"After what we been through, who's a-scared of dyin'?"
she demanded. She waved an arm. "It's the place, here.
It's what we was buildin' here. You know that's gone."

"I know. I been on that side of it, their side," he admit-
ted. "But we . . . you and me . . . we ain't finished."

"Ho! How do we start over, if we live?"

"We made friends," he said. "Wrong side, but the Kovacses and them."

She softened. "Never had friends before. Adam . . . he
was a kinda friend. Honest and square and all."

"They were onto us," he said. "When they brought in
the first gunnies they got onto us. Thing is, Kovacs and
them, they didn't turn their backs."

"Uh-huh. And what about Buchanan?"

"I dunno."

"Where'd you get to know him?"

"Texas way. Long ago, afore I got into the pen. I was
ridin' . . . you know. He wasn't wearin' a badge or nothin'.
Just helpin' out a friend, a rancher."

"He fought agin you?"

"Wasn't much of a scrap. We run away. Two of our
boys went over. Buchanan, he's tough and you know what
I mean. Tougher'n two boots."

"You think he may be one of . . . them?"

"Cattle Association? No, I don't believe so."

"But he could be a spy?"

"Ain't his dish. But we got to watch him."

"Don't trust nobody, nohow, no time," she said tightly.
"We got this far, we can't let down no rails."

"Right," said her husband.

"And what about Trevor?"

"Never did know any Britisher afore."

"He sure talks funny."

"Yea, he ain't got the language down good. But he
never was like Crane nor Fox. Different breed of cat."

"Him a bachelor, he never did make no grabs for me,"
she said. "You noted?"

"I noted."

She grinned and leaned a shoulder against his and said
huskily, "I never did nothin' to deserve a man like you."

"Huh. Reckon I was the lucky one."

"Gettin' late, honey. Can't we go to bed?"

He returned the pressure of her shoulder. "You bet,
baby. I'll attend the stable."

She went into the house. It was a simple, plain shack,

but she had managed dimity curtains and Navajo rugs. She began to undress, smiling to herself in anticipation.

Rob came in fast. "Pack some duds. Food, the guns and shells. Whatever we got."

"Why? . . . What?"

"Fire. Over Trevor's way."

"Fire?" It was a frightening word in that country.

"A big damn blaze. And my barn shotgun's missin, the one with my initials carved onto it."

"My God." In their experience, they were quickly aware of the implication. Adam Day had been framed, now it was their turn. She flung her Levis back on and yanked at her boots. Then she said, "Somebody's been here. You know my silk rebozo? The one you got me in Juarez? It's gone."

"Yeah, sure. You got that side o' bacon. Let's make a big package."

"The dirty bastards," she said, moving quickly to obey.

"Sure. Has to be somethin' anybody'd know is ourn. Just like they done Adam, they're tryin' to stick somethin' up ours. You get over to Kovacs, hear?"

"Not alone."

He said, "Look, nothin's gonna be left here. Nothin', you hear me? I gotta get to town. Buchanan and Trevor. I got to ride with them."

She was making a swift bundle of basic possessions, clothing wrapped in bedding. She went into the kitchen and wrapped cold meat and newly baked bread and a side of bacon. "Make a pack for little Tony, he'll carry it. You take Gray. I'll take Red and the pack. We'll go first to Kovacs. . . ."

"Hell," he said, "Trevor mightn't know he's bein' burned out."

She slumped. "Hadn't thought on that. You're right, Rob. Only . . . if anything should happen to you and I ain't there . . . I'd die, I swear I'd die."

He hugged her tight, fiercely, kissed her on the mouth. "You and me, Fay, you and me. Now, let's git movin'."

He saw to his revolver. He packed two rifles and several

boxes of ammunition. He had a derringer and a Smith and Wesson .44 double action, a new pistol. It was the one habit he could not shake, being prepared with guns and bullets.

Tony was a willing, small worker. The mounts were as named, a gray and a chestnut-red. Once their minds were made up, the Whelans moved like a trained team. In a very few minutes, they were mounted with Tony on a lead line.

They sat a moment looking at the modest house, looking out over the fields past the barn, the pasture where the cattle were scattered. They would not see that little herd again, they knew. They had tried; they had done their best, and now it was to be taken away from them.

They wasted no words. They were aware in their simple fashion that they had done their best in this place. There was nothing left to do but put up a fight for survival.

4

Trevor had driven a buckboard to town. Buchanan heard only a few words of Whelan's message before he began to pack his belongings.

Trevor said, "But we've always been friendly, Rob. How could anyone possible believe you would burn me out?"

Whelan shrugged. "You know the name they give us. You been friendly, sure. Five'll get you a hundred they lay it on Fay and you."

"No! How beastly can they be?"

Buchanan said, "Whelan knows."

"I know," said Whelan. "I been there and back."

They hustled to the livery stable. It was past midnight. Buchanan lashed his soogans in the buckboard, Whelan rode off. Trevor brought out a pair of matched bays. Buchanan helped him hitch them up.

Trevor said, "They move fast, what? Never quite knew I was associating with such people, y' know. Rough country and all that, but nothing like this I assure you."

"Let's get on the road," said Buchanan. "If Whelan runs into any of 'em, the killin' will start right there."

They mounted the buckboard, and Trevor picked up the reins. He had good hands, Buchanan saw at once, he knew his horses. He took the team out, let them warm up before he broke them into a trot. They wanted to run when they were on the road for the home ranch.

They were very swift. Buchanan clung onto the seat, his rifle in one hand. Everything had indeed happened with astonishing speed since his awful vision of Adam hanging from the roadside tree. Colonel Bradbury could never have acted in this manner, without careful planning, with the animal violence required for such deeds. There were forces within forces, more brains than were in the head of either Bradbury or Morgan Crane.

Not that it mattered. The worst had happened; this was war and the lines were clearly drawn. Like Whelan, he had seen range wars before. It was civil strife, there was nothing worse in the West. Murder in the name of injustice was part of it. A scarlet wind blew over Wyoming, and soon he saw the reflection against the sky.

Trevor drove like a man in a race. When he turned off the main road, he guided the buckboard over rough terrain with consummate skill. The odor of smoke was around them now, and the fire was dying. It was too late to save anything, Buchanan knew. Trevor was cleaned out as only flames could manage it.

They came into the yard and pulled up. The horses snorted, and Buchanan went to their heads, knowing their fear of fire. Whelan came from the ruins of the stable. Trevor ran to the house, which was ghostly, the walls standing awkwardly crooked in the starlight.

Whelan called, "Stay away. It'll collapse on you any minute."

They gathered and watched the dying flames. Buchanan asked, "Any sign?"

"Oh, sure. Two horses. Me and Fay, we always ride together. They took my shotgun and her rebozo along. They'll be showin' it all over town, claimin' Trevor made a grab for Fay and she got mad and we burned him out."

"They drag the other sign?"

"Yep. Not too good, neither. They ain't real smart."

Trevor sighed. "The house was too good for burnin'. Modeled it after my brother's country place in Hampshire. Shame, isn't it?"

"Damn shame," said Buchanan. "They turn loose the stock?"

"Yeah. Even them coyotes wouldn't burn a horse in a barn," said Whelan. "I dabbed onto the stallion and that big buckskin devil. All I could find."

"Saddles?"

"You do think of things. Got a couple was hangin' on the corral rails."

Buchanan turned to Trevor. "You happen to have a smokehouse?"

"Why, yes."

"Load the buckboard with all the food you can find. We can ride the horses."

"But to what place? Where?" asked Trevor.

"Kovacs' place," said Whelan. "It's solid."

"Know a trail around town that'll get us there?" asked Buchanan.

"Certain."

"Best be at it. They're bound to go for Whelan's spread next."

"We knowed that when we seen the fire," said Whelan.

"What about the other farmers, small ranchers?"

"Wouldn't bet on 'em," Whelan shrugged. "It ain't in 'em. They hang to their own places. If they don't see it happen—they believe it won't happen to them."

They went about their tasks. They were ready to leave

when Dan Badger rode in on the mule, unmistakable against the starlit sky."

"Saw the fire," he said. "Got here soon enough to track 'em in."

"Who were they?" asked Trevor.

"Pollard and that laughin' devil, Dorn. Toad Tanner and Dab Geer. Them two new ones was on the stage with Amanda and Buchanan."

"But none of the ranchmen."

"Course not. They hire. New ones come in on the stage agin. More will be comin'. Hired guns. Country full o' scallywags."

"You ridin' with us?"

"To the Kovacs' place?"

"It's where the fight'll be," said Buchanan.

"Like you say." Badger nodded. "Me and them afore me, we didn't open God's country for men like these to hog it, to kill other folks. Some of us had a vision, we seen it is the promised land. Everything's here, all good. Better the Injuns kept it for themselves, so sez I."

They loaded the buckboard and drove over dark, back ways, slow and careful. They passed through three small farms and a ranch and told the story. They were met with suspicion, they were met with fear and trembling. No one joined them despite dire warning. Each family clung to its homestead.

On the last leg of their journey, Buchanan remarked, "Some of them will sell out. Some of them will run. The rest'll suffer like you, Trevor, from the fire."

"I see it now. It is new to me. The rustling, that always went on. There have been lynchings. I knew about them, but it was not my business. It was something I did not approve, but Judge Lynch is strong in cattle country. I've been wrong."

"One man can't do much," Buchanan told him. "Right up to when Bradbury sent for me there had to be some feelin' that things could be worked out. He knows me. No, it's a force of evil. Once begun, it spreads like prairie fire."

"I should've acted, y' know. The gov'nor, someone in Washington. I should've tried."

"You paid your dues tonight," Buchanan said. "Now it's can-we-live-through-it?"

"But you need not. It is not your war."

Buchanan said sadly, "Might say that. On the other hand, I saw the man Adam strung up to that tree. I saw what I didn't like in town. Maybe it wasn't mine, but it sure has got to be somethin' I can't walk away from. Didn't take long, neither."

"Quite," said Trevor. "Nasty business, but here we are and all that."

"You been here long?"

"Long enough to think of it as my country, y' see."

"Ah, yes. That's a heap o' time, figure it that way."

"Younger son," said Trevor, smiling gently. "Family's rolling in it. Sent me out here to establish myself and fortune. Didn't expect much. Fooled 'em."

"Could be you lost it all."

"Not to be worried about. Start again."

"If you live." Buchanan was curious.

"Oh, yes. Life, eh? A lease on something not ever permanent, now, isn't it?"

Buchanan was satisfied. "You'll do to take along. Let's get to the Kovacs' spread and make some plans."

They were a tight little caravan, Whelan, the tall mule carrying Badger, the lead horse, the buckboard, all traveling to a rendezvous with violence.

Coco Bean rode the stage with growing trepidation. Jackson, the driver, had greeted him in Billings, recognizing him, tellin him that Buchanan was looking for him.

"They ain't give me a shotgun. You could ride with me."

Coco shuddered away from the proffered, wicked weapon. "Guns! Don't want no guns. Don't ever come to me with no gun."

Jackson stared. "Buchanan said you was a fighter."

Coco held up two hard, round fists like cannonballs. "You see them? They fight. They fight real good. They knocked me out a big ole miner in Butte. No guns. Them!"

"See whatcha mean," said Jackson hastily. He climbed up and shoved the shotgun into a boot fitted for that purpose. "Okay. If you a friend of Buchanan, reckon you're all right. C'mon up here if y' like."

Coco climbed up, shoving his portmanteau onto the top of the stage with other luggage. There were five men squeezed into the tonneau of the stage. None of them looked like good company. Coco was wearing Levis, tight around his formidable legs, walking boots, a hickory shirt, and a round hard hat. His glad rags were in the bag. He had learned that when meeting Buchanan he must be ready for emergencies, and this already loomed as another of those bad times where guns were involved. He had a mortal fear and hatred of all kinds of guns.

Jackson gathered up the ribbons. Gauging in the wind, he spat tobacco juice over his shoulder, missing the luggage, missing the stagecoach. "Them fellers below there? Hired guns. Comin' to help the big ranchers."

"Guns," said Coco dispiritedly. "Had I the sense the Lord gave a duck, I would git down from here right now."

"Seen a man lynched, mighty near. Your friend Buchanan, he's agin the big ranchers, seems like."

"Uh-huh. Right smack in the midst of it all." Coco did not need to be told. He had been following Buchanan around for a long time, hoping to settle the issue of who was the better man with his fists. Something to do with guns always interfered. Usually Buchanan managed to catch a bullet some place in his big carcass.

Jackson said, "There's doin's around Buffalo. Ain't heard the latest, but we'll soon know. . . . Up there, Dan, Tom, let's take 'em out. Gee, now!"

It was not a long trip in miles from Billings to Buffalo, but it seemed ages as Coco worried atop the stage. He was a proud but humble man who was a holy terror in the prize ring and a lamb outside the squared circle. He had done well in the West since meeting Buchanan in an El Paso Texas Ranger jail. If it were not for all the shooting . . .

On the other hand, he knew Buchanan did not solicit trouble, indeed, did his best to avoid it. They had enjoyed some rare times, laughs and peace together. Much as he might want to be elsewhere, when Buchanan was in trouble, Coco must hie himself thence.

He brooded all the way to the stage station in Buffalo. There he rescued his luggage and descended, looking up and down a street deserted of casual strollers. Jackson had pointed out the hotel. He went toward it.

The lobby was deserted. He put down his bag and frowned, hearing voices from the back of the hotel. He moved uncertainly toward a door, which was closed.

He heard a man's voice cry out, "All right! All right! Don't hit me again."

"Buchanan went out with Trevor, right?"

"Yes . . . yes . . ." The man was in agony.

"Buchanan took his luggage, right?"

"Yes."

"That's it," said another voice. "Buchanan's sidin' them. It figured thataway."

"Should we kill this one?"

"He didn't want to talk," said the other voice. Coco tried the door. It opened. He edged it, scowling. It seemed to him that someone was hurting a friend of Buchanan's. He applied his eye to the crack.

Someone held a one-legged man against the wall. Another was holding a revolver with which he had been striking the crippled man, whose face was bleeding, whose expression of pain and fear was too much for Coco's sense of justice.

He rammed open the door, flew across the room. He hit the man with the gun and knocked him flat as a flounder. He grabbed for the other man.

Something struck him across the back of the neck. He went down on hands and knees. A boot kicked him in the ribs. Another foot reached him from the one who had been holding the crippled man.

Coco had not reckoned on the third man, who had not spoken, who had been behind the door. Now they put the boots to him in turn. Before he passed out he heard one say, "A black sonofabitch at that."

When he awakened, he was in a jail cell. He lay on a

hard pallet and had difficulty in breathing. One leg was doubled under him. His face was puffed, his eyes almost closed. He had great difficulty in sitting up.

Bars divided two cells. In the other was the one-legged man, blood drying on his face.

"Name of Weevil," he croaked. "Thanks for tryin' to help."

Coco's voice also creaked. They had struck him across the throat during the methodical beating. "You're welcome. Lotta good it did."

"They'd a shot me," Weevil told him. "Now they got a better idea. They're gonna get us lynched."

"Who is they?"

"Pollard, Dorn, and Tanner is who you seen. They work for the Cattleman's Association, they calls it."

"Buchanan?"

"You know Buchanan?"

"I was lookin' for him."

"Man, you are in Dutch. Buchanan's agin 'em. He's out there some place with Jack Trevor and mebbe a few others. There's an army agin 'em."

"This here place gone crazy?"

"Just about."

"You said lynch us. What for?"

"Consortin' with outlaws. Buchanan, Trevor, all the people with 'em have been declared outlaws."

"Consortin'," mused Coco. "Uh-huh. Only we ain't been, have we?"

"Don't matter to them. They like to lynch people. Say it's a lesson. Shows who owns the country."

"Uh-huh. Me and Buchanan, we seen a lot of people want to own what ain't rightly theirs. Come to a bad end, all of 'em."

"You and Buchanan never seen an army like they got here," said Weevil dully. "They even cut the telegraph wire so nobody can get to the capital or any place like o' that."

"It sounds right evil," said Coco. "It sounds like Tom Buchanan will get his dander up."

"He ain't never been up against nothin' like this."

Coco lay back down. He hurt all over. He thought his leg might be broken. "Uh-huh. And they never been up agin anybody like Tom Buchanan."

He had never been hurt this bad, he knew. It was a tremendous shock. He could talk brave to the one-legged man, but he had seen lynchings in the South, he knew all about them. And he was so bad hurt he wouldn't be able to punch it out with them when they came, to make them shoot him. It would be like stickin' pigs, and he had always loathed that time of year back on the plantation when he had been a slave boy.

The Kovacs' house was staunch, but pitifully few were gathered there. Too many women, Buchanan thought. Not enough men to man the windows.

Then at noon two riders came in on work horses. They were tall and skinny, with prominent Adam's apples. They were father and son, name of Thorne.

The old man was gray-haired, his pale eyes washed out. The son was a younger edition of the father. They carried old Remingtons and a pouch of ammunition.

"Badger, he tole us about it," said Pa Thorne. "Knew we'd be in for it, we're on Bar-B land. Knew the richuns would be after us. Always are, wherever you go."

"Ain't no place to run," said Sonny Thorne. "Brought some cornpone and jerky and a couple hams. Reckon they'll git the rest of our hawgs."

Kovacs explained, "Is pig farmers." He did not seem pleased.

Buchanan was not favorably impressed, but anyone who could shoot was welcome. The windows would have to be double-manned against a possible charge. There was always the fire hazard, and the enemy had proved itself fond of setting fires. Then there was the question of casualties. . . . There was no way to avoid it.

The women served food. There seemed enough for a short siege, but there were many mouths to feed. Water from the creek was stored in every possible receptacle. The creek ran nearby, but it would be under sharpshooter attack when the siege began.

There was no possibility that there would not be a siege,
Buchanan knew. The ranchers had to attack, they had
begun with the hanging of Adam Day and gone on to burn
out Jack Trevor. There was no turning back for them,
they were into it and had to finish it. He had been through
it before, one way or another. He meant to make every
preparation, to advise everyone to stay put in this strong
stone building . . . and to say their prayers.

He prowled the ample big-room with its three narrow,
high windows, two on the front, one on the side opposite
the fireplace. The door was thick, seasoned wood on heavy
hinges. It was defensible.

There was a hall leading to the kitchen where there
were two similar windows and a rear door. The two big
bedrooms led off the hall, each with one window. All
would be manned by shooters with rifles.

People milled about, visiting, a change from their ordinary day to day existence. There was a holiday air, which
would soon enough be dissipated.

Buchanan heard voices in the kitchen. Trevor was
speaking to Amanda Day.

Trevor was saying painfully, "But surely, dear lady,
you cannot believe that I had any hand in the murder of
your husband?"

"That is for you to decide," she answered coldly.

"It was upon that rock that I split from the others of the
Cattleman's Association." Now he spoke with dignity.

"Too late to save Adam."

"Yes. Too late." Trevor sighed. "I can only crave your
forgiveness."

"A man like Buchanan arrives too late, but had he been
here, it would not have happened."

"You may be correct. He moves quickly and with skill."

"I must prepare more food," she said, her accents still
icy.

Trevor wandered into the hallway. He peered at Buchanan. He said, "A beautiful lady. Beautiful."

"I noted," said Buchanan. "Give her time."

"Time? Eh? What?"

"Been around a lot," Buchanan said. "Man's voice gives him away sometimes."

"I say, now. Really, that's a bit much."

"Uh-huh," said Buchanan. "Scuse me all to pieces."

He went into the kitchen. Amanda was cutting bacon. She did everything with grace. He wondered what kind of a man the farmer Adam Day had been when she met him. Not the same man who was hanged, he knew.

She looked at him, and her face softened. "Are you hungry?"

"Always, ma'am. Good thing I don't eat every time. I'd be bigger'n a house."

"Never," she denied. "Not you."

He accepted a sandwich of bread and cold meat. "Heard you talkin' with Jack Trevor."

She frowned again. "They burnt him out, but does that make him one of us?"

"Depends on what you mean by *us*. Seems to me we got pushed here together, willy-nilly. Can't expect us to be all alike."

"Trevor is landed gentry. Noble birth and all that."

"Can't hold that against him."

"I don't trust him."

"Your privilege, ma'am. Thing is, he can shoot, and we need shooters."

"You're very sure of that, aren't you?"

"Man can see a storm brewin' if he knows the country."

"You believe in people, don't you, Buchanan?"

"Some." He chewed on the sandwich. The lady had recovered quickly from the hanging of her husband.

"And you can be exasperating."

"Uh-huh." There would be trouble outside and trouble inside, no question about that. Amanda Day was not a woman to reserve opinions.

Raven came into the kitchen. She moved with light grace, but there was something about her, something not quite full-blooded Crow. He swallowed and spoke to her.

"Your people in the hills?"

"These are my people," she replied gravely. "Jenny. Pieter."

"But the Crows. Are they the peacable tribe?"

"Ask Badger. He knows."

"Uh-huh." He finished the sandwich. The girl was as ret-
icent as most Indians, but she seemed utterly devoted to
Pieter and Jenny Kovacs. There were good Indians and
bad Indians and good white people and bad white people,
and sometimes he thought there were more bad whites. He
decided to forget about Raven for the time being. If she
wanted to stay and take a chance on dying with the white
people who had raised her, that was none of his business.

He went to the door and opened it, scanning the horizon. The lush and lovely countryside lay fallow in the af-
ternoon sun. It was good land. It was the kind of place
over which people fought.

The tall mule came into sight, running, the mountain
man swaying with the rhythm. Buchanan closed the door
behind him and went to meet Badger.

"Whoa, now." The deepset eyes peered down at Buchanan. "You ken a black man name o' Coco Bean?"

"I do."

"Jackson, the stage driver, he give me word."

"Uh-huh?"

"Stage loaded with gunmen. Comin' in by the dozens."

"About Coco."

"Yeah. He's in the jail."

"Whatever for?"

"Could be 'cause he allowed as how you're his friend."

"It's that bad already? Any friend of mine is in trouble?"

"Worse'n that. Weevil's jailed, too. They're plannin' on
lynchin' the two of 'em."

Buchanan started for the corral and the big horse.
Badger followed him.

"Nighttime," said the mountain man. "They allus do
their foul deeds at night. Got to drink a lotta likker and
all. Got to talk a lot, make theirselves believe."

"Right."

"Reckon we go in, eh?"

"I go in. Coco's my friend."

"Got to know the way. Let it get dark."

Buchanan hesitated. "You know a way?"

"Ridin' around, an old man like me, he gets to know."

"Just the two of us?"

"Mebbe."

"Trevor?"

"Mebbe. Two horses and the Britisher would give us a better outlook, sorta."

"Dynamite?"

"Jail ain't that hefty. Might hurt 'em. Your friend and Weevil is already beat bad."

"They beat Coco?"

"Did so, says Jackson."

Buchanan said, "Coco's a gentle soul. Nobody should hurt Coco."

"Don't git too mad," said Badger. " 'Tain't good fer what we're gonna do."

"A thick rope," said Buchanan.

"Yep. My idee exackly."

Trevor came from the house, curious. Buchanan told him the latest bad news.

Trevor said, "Oh my, yes. When do we start?"

They started at twilight. They led two horses and carried a coil of heavy rope borrowed from Kovacs. They rode into the dark, going around the town behind Badger and the tireless big mule. They carried rifles and revolvers, and Trevor had a keen hunting knife from Sheffield in England, the best of steel.

There were few stars. Badger brought them by a devious path through heavy undergrowth, past the smelly town dump. They crossed behind the buildings facing the main street.

The noise from the Powder River and the Deuces Wild saloons was reaching a peak. Buchanan heard his name mentioned a half-dozen times. Curses were called down upon Trevor. Kovacs was not ignored, nor the Whelans.

Pollard was heard to yell, "We got pos'tive proof the Whelans burned out Trevor. They're all dogs. They got to be treated like dogs."

"Trevor messin' with Whelan's woman," roared Morgan Crane. "No good British whoremaster."

Trevor nudged Buchanan, who nodded. Badger sat on the mule and shook his head. They went around behind the jail, which was a wooden building, not much more than a shack. There had been little use for a strong hoosegow up until now. It was staunch enough for overnight drunks or vagrants, no more.

There were two barred windows, high up. Buchanan reined his horse close to the wall of the jailhouse and spoke into its ear for a moment, calming it. Then he gingerly climbed upon the saddle, bracing himself against the wall while Trevor held the bridle. There was glass, which he did not want to break for fear of alarming the jailers, who might be sober. He managed to get out his Barlow, open it, and attack the putty. He removed the glass and handed it down to Badger.

Coco's voice came from the darkness within, soft and confident. "That you, Tom?"

"It ain't Santa Claus," said Buchanan. "How you doin' in there?"

"Wantin' out, mainly."

"How's Weevil?"

"He's bad. But they give him his leg back."

"Where's it hurt most?"

"Thought they broke my leg. Guess not altogether. Banged up my ribs good, though."

"You got any power left?"

"How much you need?"

"Might need a shove against this wall."

"You need it . . . I better have it. They gonna hang us, Tom."

"Yeah. So I hear." Badger was handing up the rope. "Grab hold of this. Pass it on to Weevil."

He got down, moved the horse to the other window. He removed that pane of glass.

"Weevil, you hear me?"

"I do."

"How many guards in there?"

"Two, three. Drinkin' a lot of booze right now."

"Sure they are. Stick your end of the rope out to me, can you? Get on the bunk or whatever."

Weevil tried, failed. The window was too high.

Buchanan hoisted himself higher. He reached his long arm inside the building. He found the end of the rope, pulled it out. He pulled until he had a loop. Then he made a tie, testing it, hoping it would stand up under strain.

Badger said, "Give it here. Ol' Muley's got the strength."

"Right." Buchanan leaned close to the window. "Coco?"

"I ain't gone no place."

"We're going to try to yank down this wall. Might need a bit of help. When you see the rope go tight, you shove, hear?"

"On the wall?"

"Not on the ceiling. You hear me, Weevil?"

"I ain't all that strong, but I'll do it."

Buchanan got down from the saddle and picked his rifle from the boot. Trevor already had his long gun cradled under one arm. Badger led the mule from the building until the line was taut.

"Might be some quick action if this works," Buchanan said.

"Right-o," Trevor replied, cheerful as always when there was action in prospect.

Badger whispered to his mule. The beast strained. The rope went to its limit, stretching, tightening. There was a small creaking sound. Nothing happened.

Buchanan said, "Stronger than I reckoned."

Coco's voice came plaintively, "C'n I stop pushin' now? It kinda hurts."

"You can rest," said Buchanan. "I ain't sure this is such a good notion."

"If we had a team," said Trevor. "Ah, well. Shall we storm the bastion?"

"You mean go around to the front door and knock polite?"

"Ah—why not be riotous? Bawdy? Loud? Drunken?"

Buchanan said, "Now, that makes sense. Badger? Can you keep that dally on the jailhouse?"

"Even so," said Badger.

"Then let's do what Trevor says." He called out, "Coco?"

"Still here."

"We're comin' in. Be ready to butt your head against that wall. Weevil . . . you use the bunk for a batterin' ram."

"You'll get us all kilt but okay, it's better'n chokin' on a rope," said Weevil.

Buchanan led the way through the alley alongside the hoosegow. Trevor trod lightly at his heels. They paused before showing themselves. The sound from the saloons had increased. Any moment now the lynch mob would muster the courage to act.

"Two, three guards," said Buchanan. "Can we make enough noise to fool 'em for a minute?"

"If they are wassailing, they are for us."

"Wassailin'," said Buchanan. "A fancy word for gettin' pie-eyed. Let's move."

They raised their voices to the sky. "This way, boys. No use to wait no longer. String 'em up."

They swept into the office of the jail. Three men were pulling at the necks of three bottles. " 'Bout time," said one. "Take 'em and damn their souls."

"Uh-huh," said Buchanan. He swept the first man down with the barrel of the rifle, slammed the head of the other against a desk. Trevor hit the third with the butt of his gun, cracking the skull, bringing blood.

Buchanan said, "Don't even need keys. These sons left the doors open for the mob."

"I believe the other sons are advancing," said Trevor.

Buchanan peered out the door. The mob was swarming from both saloons, joining in the middle of the street. The night air was polluted by shouts of drunken threat.

Buchanan said, "Hope that old mule can pull with us helpin'. Otherwise we might be in a mite of a fight."

"Carry on," said Trevor.

They ran into the cells. Weevil had the bunk loose and was pushing it against the wall. Coco was groaning, but his shoulder was ready when Buchanan went past him like a freight train, shouting as he went, "Badger! Kick it!"

Trevor was slight, but he could seize the end of the bunk in Weevil's cell and use it as a battering ram. Buchanan shouted once more, and they all hit the wall at once.

There was a grinding sound. Nails screeched, leaving lumber. Buchanan smashed at the wall with all his might and main. Coco bent to the task, grimacing with pain.

And outside, the tall mule made one more effort. The wall began to give, slowly at first. Buchanan leaned back, then hit it again with the weight and the strength of two men. The wall toppled, not without dignity, grudgingly slapping to earth.

Coco gasped, "I'm about beat, Tom."

"Get to a horse. Trevor will help. . . . Weevil, you're an old wrangler. Can you ride?"

"Anything that's got hair on it." The hotel man hobbled over the fallen ruins of the wall.

"Badger! Get 'em mounted," called Buchanan. "People seem to be comin' in."

Trevor had already sent one shot crackling down the corridor outside the cells. Buchanan saw Pollard duck and run, yelling for horses as he foresaw the pursuit. It would be a running retreat, Buchanan thought, shooting low, knocking down a man over whom others tumbled.

He said, "Got it blocked. Let us make tracks."

"Right-o." They ran for the horses. Badger and the rescued pair were already galloping into the night. "No fun shootin' ducks on a pond, eh?"

They leaped into the saddles. Now men were shooting at them, and silhouetted against a starry sky, they were good targets. Buchanan paused to empty the magazine of his Remington into the motley crew of attackers, thankful for the booze they had put away to the detriment of their aim.

Trevor was riding. In the distance, they could see the three horsemen ahead of them.

"You know the back ways?" asked Buchanan.

"Not so well as our mountain man."

"Then keep him in sight."

Buchanan dropped back. Trevor hesitated, saw the reasoning behind Buchanan's order, went on. Alone Buchanan waited. One horseman appeared, then another.

He fired at them. The first man went down. The second veered off wildly, reined around, and rode helter-skelter back into the town.

Buchanan rode. He could see Trevor ahead. If worse came to worse, he thought, he could find his way back to Kovacs' place. He was a plainsman, he could retrace any course he had once traversed.

No other horsemen appeared. He spurred into the night. They would not risk his gunfire now. They knew well his destination. Cool heads would restrain all but a drunken, headstrong few, he thought. Tomorrow it would begin.

Tomorrow the siege would be laid. The Cattleman's Association could wait no longer. It would be their sincere endeavor to do away with all witnesses of what had thus far taken place. They would know that the Kovacs' house was the logical point of last defense for the people of the Wyoming plains.

5

Coco's ribs were broken. Fever set in due to the hard ride from town. Buchanan was worried by the sight of his friend's sunken eyes and by his muddled muttering.

Raven went out into the night with a small, sharp knife. When she returned, her arms were laden with certain plants from the fields behind the house. Dan Badger worked with her over the stove, preparing a poultice and a steaming gruel. Coco lay in the Kovacs' bed and breathed with greater ease, slumbering.

Badger looked over Weevil's wounds and found them painful but superficial. "He's an old man, tough but a bit

feeble. Put him on blankets in thar with Coco. Wish we
hadn't made 'em bang down that wall."

"Saved their lives," Buchanan said.

"But now we know they'll be after us by mornin', eh?"
Trevor was calm as always. Sometimes he seemed a bit
too cheerful, perhaps.

Buchanan said, "They'll be gatherin', all right. It won't
be any joke. It's an army they're puttin' together."

The others were silent. Raven moved about, watching
Coco, attending to Weevil as he groaned at every motion
of his aching body. It was a pitiful group, Buchanan
thought. There seemed no way they could prevail.

He went outside. There was no sound but the chirping
of insects, the song of birds, and the ripple of the nearby
creek. The stone barn was close to the house, which, he
knew, could be good or bad as the case might be.

Dan Badger joined him. "Right nice night, ain't it?"

"Just fine."

"Got me a cabin up in Crow country. Got an old Sharps
that's oiled and ready. Got lead and powder. I'll be moseyin' along for now."

"But you'll be back."

"That gun'll shoot straight and far. Hate to use it on
people. Comes the time a man has to take a side."

"You and me, we got no stake here," said Buchanan.
"Save only one: folks shouldn't be ground down for reasons of greed."

"You savvy, Tom Buchanan. The Lord looks down."

"And thanks for takin' care of Coco," Buchanan said.

"A black brother. Jim Beckwourth was my friend afore
he went over. A good man. Plenty black men in the old
days. People don't know."

"There's whole heaps that people don't know." Buchanan sighed deeply.

There was the sound of a wagon approaching. Buchanan's hand dropped to his gun butt. Badger faded from
sight like a ghost in the night.

A voice bellowed, "Halooo the house. It's me. Durkin."

The door opened behind Buchanan, and he moved

quickly out of the light thrown from within. Trevor stepped into the dimness, rifle in hand. ·

"Bull Durkin?"

The wagon came closer. The loud voice called, "Got the news from Jackson. Been travelin' since sunset. Cactus and Sutter is with me."

"What do you want?" Trevor's voice was harsh.

"To come in. That you, Trevor?"

"It is, indeed. Why should you come here?"

The springs of the wagon creaked, and a man came into the light. Inside the house, people crowded the door and the two front windows. Trevor held the rifle steady.

The man was no more than five feet seven inches tall. He was as wide as a barn door. His arms hung to his knees. He had a wide face and a protruding jaw. He looked—he looked like a bull, Buchanan thought.

"I come because I caught them damn rustlers this mornin'." The man's conversational voice come from the deep chest like a foghorn on the river. "Tried to tell Dealer Fox. He put ten men on me, run me off. They lynched Adam, they gone too far."

"But you're not in it," said Trevor. "You're up in the hills, on the high plain."

"I ain't in it now," said Durkin. "You wanna bet I wouldn't be in it when they clean yawl out?"

Trevor half turned to Buchanan. "He's a wild one. Fights everyone, including the association. I can't guarantee him."

Buchanan stepped into the light. "Bull, when did you turn rancher?"

"Buchanan. Heard you was around. This here time we are on the same side." Durkin's voice was not friendly, but it sounded respectful.

"They ran you out of New Mexico. You still hangin' rustlers?"

"Strung up two this mornin'," said Durkin doggedly. "Think on it. Because of them, Adam Day got lynched, this war is made possible. Nobody'd believe me agin the association, that blames the rustlin' on the settlers."

"But you beat a nester and ran him off your graze," Trevor said. "Didn't you, now?"

"Another settin' of a nest," Durkin growled. "Buchanan'll tell you, this here's a war to the finish. I may be rough, but I ain't no damn fool. Never could git along with Fox and them. It's fish or cut bait, and I'm here to fish for them gunnies bein' brought in."

Trevor, uncertain, asked, "What do you think, Buchanan?"

"First, I better tell you, Bull, there's another couple of guns on you. Just in case."

"Be pretty dumb if there wasn't." He held up empty hands. "You need me and you need Cactus and Sutter."

Buchanan said, "There's the barn. Cactus and Sutter could hold out there."

"Okay," said Durkin. "I got ammunition and food in the wagon. I got blankets, everything we could grab onto."

"One bad move, Bull," said Buchanan. "Just one. Then it'll be you and me. Right?"

Durkin grinned. His teeth were jagged. "Ain't never tried you yet. If'n I do, you'll know it."

"I'll know it, all right. And you won't forget it."

"Suits me." Durkin turned and bawled, "Git the wagon into the barn, there. Feed the hosses and turn 'em loose. No use to git 'em kilt right off. Bed down."

Cactus and Sutter were hard-bitten riders, no more, no less, Buchanan saw. They obeyed without question. Both wore their holsters tied low on their flanks. No doubt they were gun hands, as Bull Durkin had been before he swung his loop wide enough and often enough to put together a herd down south. It was a touchy situation, but there seemed no other course than to accept aid at face value.

Durkin followed his men. Badger slid out of the deep shadows as Trevor came close to Buchanan.

"The association lynched Adam Day. He lynched the rustlers this very day," Badger said. "Watch him."

"Wouldn't trust the man across the creek," said Trevor.

"So long as we know all that," Buchanan told them. "When the attack comes, we'll know a lot more. If him or one of his men prove wrong—kill 'em."

"I don't like it," Trevor murmured. "I don't like it at all, y' know."

Badger said, "May the good Lord protect you." Then he was gone, and the sound of the mule running was fading in the night.

Trevor said, "Perhaps we should have sent him for help?"

"Whereabouts? With the telegraph wire down, it would take days to get enough help here. And you know the association's got political power."

Trevor shrugged. "Right-o. We make the best of it, then."

"Better check on 'em." Buchanan went into the house.

Whelan was unhappy. "Buchanan, you know that bastard . . . 'scuse me, ladies, but that's what he is . . . we oughta run him off right now."

"And have a shootout before the war even starts up?"

"He's no good."

"Is so," said Kovacs. "A bad man."

The women were silent, but now Pa Thorne spoke up.

"Yawl went into town and picked up a wornout old one-legged coot and a nigger."

"Uh-huh." Buchanan was patient, but time was running on his forbearance.

"I swan to ginney, that's might peculiar goin's on."

"You do, huh?"

"Vittles bein' short enough. Them two won't be no help."

"You think so." He swallowed hard, containing himself.

"You got the nigger in a bed. Where I come from, he'd be on the floor and glad of it."

"I see. Where you come from. Hog Land?"

"Mississippi, by Gawd. Where a nigger's a black nothin'."

"And you were a slave owner?"

Thorne was taken aback. "Who, me? I didn't own pot nor winder. We come out here after ma died, Sonny and me. Scrabbled to git a homestead and some hawgs."

"Looks like you been around 'em long enough to act like one," Buchanan snapped.

"Whut you say? Whut's that?"

"Coco is my friend. Understand that. Get it into your thick head, Mr. Thorne. Get it good."

"A nigger is yore friend?" The pig farmer was aghast.

"What's more he could take you in one hand and your son in the other and crack you like walnuts. But he wouldn't. He wouldn't take advantage of trash like you." Buchanan took a breath, seeking control. "Coco's like me, a peaceable man. I know you're ignorant, which is some sort of excuse, but Mister, you walk careful around me and don't let me hear you call Coco a nigger, not ever. You hear me?"

The man said, "Goddlemighty, Mr. Buchanan, I didn't go for to make you all that mad."

"Uh-huh," said Buchanan. "Did it, though, didn't you?"

"Uh, well, I hear you." The hog farmer retreated.

Amanda exhaled. She said, "Well, that was quite a lecture. But about Bull Durkin, now. He is a dangerous character."

Fay Whelan said, "He made a run at me once. Had to pull down on him. I swear, hawg farmers, stove up people. We are in a fix."

"How come you trust the rest of us?" asked Buchanan.

Rob Whelan interposed. "We know about you. You got to remember, Fay and me, we've had to stand by each other. Maybe we got some to learn. But we only know we got each other. Maybe we won't even have a house when this is over. Maybe we'll be dead."

"Like Badger says, only the good Lord knows," Buchanan said.

"One thing," said Fay.

"Uh-huh." Everybody wanted something, and they all came to Buchanan.

"Rob and me, we go together. You're the boss here so far as we're concerned. But don't try to separate us."

"No reason to do that." He was relieved.

"Way it is with us," Rob said. "One goes, t'other won't know how to cut it."

"Okay and good luck." He gestured. "How about standin' guard out there awhile?"

"Fine with us."

They went off into the night, prowling, never more than a few yards apart. They had come a long way together, Buchanan thought. They had scrambled for a place in life. Rob was right: even if they survived, they might lose it all and be forced to begin all over again. What they had put together was really themselves. Perhaps that was enough. He found himself staring at the high ceiling of the big room. He went outdoors and saw there was a stone parapet around the edge of the roof.

He went back inside and called to Kovacs. "Hey, is there a trapdoor to the roof?"

"Is so. In closet."

The closets were in the hallway between the kitchen and the main room. Buchanan asked, "You got a ladder?"

"Is so." Kovacs opened a closet door. There was a sturdy wooden ladder leading upward. Everything about the Kovacs property was staunch.

Buchanan said, "That trap's too tight for me. Hey, you, Sonny Thorne. Take a look up there."

The skinny man went up the steps, removed the trap. "Good roof," he called down. "Hard to set afire, I reckon. Should I git some water up here in case?"

"You do that," said Buchanan. "Leave that ladder right where it is. We'll keep a gun up there."

He walked around, examining every detail of the house and its furnishings. Amanda Day followed him, watching.

In the main bedroom, he made certain Coco and Weevil were sleeping. In the other bedroom, she spoke to him.

"You think of everything, don't you?"

"I try, ma'am." He sat down on a chair, weary of a sudden. "Wish there was some way to get yawl out of here."

"But we belong here."

"Sure, you do. Only there's a heap of guns will say you got to get out."

"You think we'd run, even if we could?"

"I think you'd be fools not to. Look, we got the Whelans and Trevor. They'll stand up. Kovacs is no fighter.

The hawg farmers—you can look at them and see what they are. Bull Durkin—we don't know yet which side he's on . . . besides his own side." He waved an arm. "Out yonder they're bringin' in an army. They got to kill us now to save their own necks."

"Of course. But you won't let them." Her coolness was amazing.

He shook his head. "Such faith no woman should have."

"Bradbury?" she asked. "He did try to buy out Adam. Could you get to him?"

"Tried that. Fox and Crane got him over a barrel. I know he was against lynchin' or he wouldn't of called for me. But right now, he's the enemy."

"Then they'll kill us." She considered. "If they do, there'll be a stench in the land, an uprising of the righteous!"

"Now, lady, don't be figurin' on martyrdom. Once in your grave, you don't count. It's a big country with plenty of room for the livin', and those who survive keep right on mindin' their own affairs. Let the dead stay buried, they figure."

"You don't believe in anything much, do you, Buchanan?" Her eyes were bright and a bit sad.

"Time and circumstance," he said. "A man does what he can. Belief? I got my beliefs."

She stood a moment staring at him. Then she went quickly from the room. He shrugged. He was not one to speak to strangers about what he believed.

He got up and went out of the house. He found the big buckskin in the corral and saddled him, spoke to him, mounted and rode out.

He rode over the terrain from which the attack must come. There were some high trees clustered at the front of the house which he would wish to have leveled if possible. There was a knoll to the west behind which the forces of the enemy could deploy in safety. Neither prospect pleased him.

He rode around for some time, squinting at his friends,

the stars under which he had so often slept. He thought about the people gathered at the Kovacs' place and how he had come among them.

He removed his hat and said a few words to his own private deity, which was not an old man with a long white beard sitting up above the clouds, but something quite closer to Buchanan and his natural surroundings.

Colonel Bradbury's *hacienda* was old-Spanish design, an elaborate place designed by Consuela, his Spanish wife of many years. She was the daughter of a consul, they had met in Austin. She was a woman of strength with deep, dark eyes; no longer young, growing heavy of body but still handsome.

Servants brought whiskey and carafes of water to the leaders of the Cattleman's Association, who were out on the patio. Torches threw light upon the scene.

Dealer Fox said, "We got those rustlers that Durkin hung, and buried them where nobody'll find them. Now we got to get Durkin."

"We're addin' up a big total," Bradbury said. He was uncomfortable, unsure.

"Pollard and them can handle it."

Morgan Crane said, "But I'm the boss in the field. I'm givin' the orders. I know how."

"Certainly, Morgan," said Fox. "Pollard and Dorn and Tanner and Geer will be your lieutenants."

Crane drank deeply. "Just make damn sure of it."

Bradbury sat back. Morgan was a fool. Fox was getting close to the deep edge, he thought. "There's women in that Kovacs' house. Four of 'em."

"What of it?" demanded Crane. "Did we send 'em there? Is it our business they gang up with the men and the guns? You think they won't shoot us quick enough?"

Bradbury said, "By God, we don't make war on women. First thing to do is palaver. Give the women time to get out."

"And have them tellin' lies all over? It's too late for that, Brad. Too late."

"And the hell with 'em," roared Crane.

"And what about when it's done?" asked Bradbury. "Then what story do we tell?"

"Our own story," said Fox.

"They're rustlers and killers. Anything we say they are. Right, Dealer?"

"That's the way it's got to be," said Fox.

"And all those men we brought in? You think they won't talk when it's over?"

"Let 'em talk. Nobody'll believe them against us. You got to realize, Brad, we are the law."

"Sure," said Crane. He tossed off another drink. "By God, that's us. The law. We own this country, we come in here and took it and made it ours."

"There can't be two sides," Fox insisted. "It's either them or us."

"Yeah, Brad, you gotta remember that."

Bradbury said, "I'm goin' to give those women a chance to get outa there."

Crane began to holler, but Fox put up a hand. "Tomorrow we'll talk about it. Dawn, ain't it? Pollard said dawn was best, like when Injuns attack. People ain't awake and ready. There's no sun to cheer 'em. Dawn."

Crane said, "And the hell with the women."

"Come on, Morgan, you've had enough to drink," said Fox. "Come on, now."

They left, Crane swaying, unsteady, his voice loud and disputatious as Fox led him to the buckboard outside the fence that surrounded the patio. Consuela came from the house and sat opposite her husband.

"You heard 'em," he said.

"You are into it very deep."

"I don't like it about the women."

"You hanged Adam Day."

"Not me. I was against that."

"You were not there to prevent it. You wished Adam Day and the other people would go away. So you hired Pollard and you have your association. And a man was hanged."

"Damn it, woman, there's nothin' I could do about it."

"I know," she said.

"What could I do? Let 'em overrun us? Give up to 'em? After all I done to build this place, this ranch?"

She smiled. "Can you see them taking it away from you? Those little people? Can you see them stealing and burning . . . and lynching?"

He stood up. He paced the patio with its imported flagstones, its high fence, its flowered paths. "There's nothin' I can do now but get the women out of there."

"They will not go," she told him.

"You don't know that."

"I would not go," she said softly.

"Like Dealer says, it's them or us."

She shook her head. "I am glad the children are away."

"You turnin' against me, Connie?" He looked despairingly at her, his hands spread. "Are you, finally?"

"No."

"But you're against what's happening."

"Yes."

"There's nothin' I can do. It's too late."

"Yes. It is too late." She arose and went into the house, closing the door behind her.

He walked back and forth, back and forth. It had all happened too fast, he told himself. There was no way he could have stopped it. He had sent for Buchanan, he had tried, knowing Buchanan's way with people.

Now they would kill Buchanan. Meaning no harm, indeed meaning well, he had brought the big man he so respected to his death.

But the women . . . He had never harmed a woman in his life.

And if he tried to interfere, if he went too far, Dealer and Crane would kill him, he saw clearly. The other members of the association would stay out of it and back up Dealer and Crane through necessity. The whole matter had got completely out of hand.

There was no escape, now. If he tried to stop the forces he had helped set in motion, he would lose wife, ranch, children, everything. He picked up the whiskey bottle and drained it.

Trevor was on watch when Buchanan rode the buckskin in. The horses would be a problem. It was best to turn loose any which could not be protected by the stone barn.

Trevor said, "Cactus and Sutter are holed up. Durkin's in the house. He'll be trouble whichever way it goes."

"Yes," said Buchanan. "Been studyin' the layout. Good to have people in the barn. The roof'll do, too, behind that stone parapet. Dangerous, but we'll have to risk it."

"Too many of 'em, right? Pick off a few. Maybe discourage 'em for a while. That's it, isn't it?"

"Uh-huh," said Buchanan. "That's the way it looks. Got to keep thinkin' on it, though. No use givin' up before the thing starts."

"Yes." He went on, "Ever been to England?"

"Not yet. Thought of Scotland sometimes. Might look up the Buchanans. And the MacNamaras."

"Filthy climate, England. Excepting this time of year. Hants is lovely this time of year."

"Hants?"

"Hampshire. Town of Romsey on the Test. One could walk across the Test in boots, but we're that way, the British. Folks have a place near Romsey."

"I see."

"Very green. 'The grass is greener on the old sod,' they say. It's very green here, now, isn't it?"

"I'd say so."

"Different hue of green. Ah, well."

"Wish you were back there?"

"Not really. 'We owe God a death.' Shakespeare, y' know. Doesn't make much difference so long as it's in a good cause. How many people just . . . die?"

"Everybody's thinkin' of dyin' around here," said Buchanan. "Me, I'm studyin' about how to live."

"Good man," said Trevor. "Right-o." He wandered away, making his rounds.

Buchanan went into the room where Coco and Weevil ing around the floor, each choosing a spot. The hog farm-

ers were together near the fireplace. The Kovacses
were in the second bedroom with the Indian girl. The
Whelans lay close together wrapped in blankets, their
guns at their sides.

Buchanan went into the room where Coco and Weevil
were awake with their pain. He unrolled his blankets,
closed the door, keeping his voice low.

"Yawl gettin' along?"

"The old man and the Injun gal," said Weevil. "They
done good for us."

Coco moistened his lips. His voice was far away. "Can't
walk around, Tom. He musta beat hard on me. I kayoed
him, but he musta hurt me more'n I knew."

Weevil said, "Sometimes he thinks it was the prizefight
where he got beat."

There was some of the gruel left in a mug. Buchanan
smelled it, choked a bit, then gave it to Coco sip by sip,
holding the round, black head in a big hand. He had become extremely fond of his friend over the years. "You
goin' to be all right. Just try and sleep."

Coco swallowed, made a face, closed his eyes. "I hit
him with two rights, Tom. He had to go down. How'd he
come to hurt me so?"

"Just sleep," Buchanan whispered.

After a moment, Coco was breathing easily, lying on his
back, hands crossed on his chest. Buchanan sat down and
removed his boots.

Weevil whispered, "He never hollered once. I hollered.
Told 'em all I know. That black man, he's dead game."

"Can you put names on those who beat him?"

"Pollard, Dorn, Tanner, Geer. Some others, maybe.
They gone loco, I swear."

"Power," said Buchanan. "Little men with power
they're not used to. They hanged a man, y' see. Made 'em
feel big."

"It's beyond me."

"Beyond ordinary understanding." He put his head
down and willed himself to sleep. For a while, it did not
work. He saw Coco being beaten, he saw Adam Day's
contorted features. His mind went to what was coming.

It was no good to dwell on it. He had covered every angle that he could conceive.

The woman had said that he didn't believe. That rankled. He wrestled with it for a few moments, then his weariness combined with his wish and he slept.

6

The Indian girl awakened Buchanan. The first pink light reflected from the mountains westward was peeking through the narrow window. He reached for his boots.

She said, "Everyone is in the house. The bad people are nearby."

"It's time." He went into the kitchen and used water to wash his hands and face, not throwing it out, saving it in case of fire. He went to the door and opened it on a crack.

The first bullet splattered against the heavy portal, and he swung it closed, and now everyone was awake in the

Kovacs' house except Coco, who slept fitfully, turning and moaning at the pain in his chest.

Buchanan said, "They'll be pepperin' the windows. Don't anybody answer their fire until I give the word. Can't waste ammunition."

He went to one of the windows at the front of the house. A shot pierced the glass, and he knocked out the rest of it with the butt of his rifle. He could see them on the knoll, and a puff of smoke came from the trees, high up, as the other window was smashed by a fusilade. He aimed at an angle, not showing himself. It was important to make them fearful right now, at the beginning. He took a deep breath. Another shot and another puff of smoke, and he pressed the trigger.

There was a yell and a crashing of branches. A man tumbled from limb to limb and lay still upon the ground.

Trevor drawled, "I say, if he wasn't killed by the bullet, the fall would've been the death of him, what?"

Durkin said from behind Buchanan, "They got high gun on us."

"The roof," Buchanan said. "Need a couple men up there."

"Right," Trevor agreed. He went nimbly up the ladder with his rifle and a box of shells.

"Now you people. Keep your heads down and watch out for ricochets. Understand?"

Durkin said, "Ain't no way of duckin' bullets, Buchanan. I say let's git out there and try 'em."

"Across open ground?"

"You ever seen what a charge can do? Scares saddle-bums like them to pieces."

"There's some sharp gunnies up there," Buchanan told him. "You want to run at 'em? Go ahead."

Durkin mumbled, "Takes more'n one. No guts around here, I kin see that."

Buchanan ignored him. The hog farmers were standing by, guns in their hands, looking a bit lost. He said to them, "You two. Go up with Trevor. Lay low and only shoot when he tells you or you see a plain target."

They were thin enough to easily squeeze through the narrow trapdoor. A bit fearfully they went, son following his father. They had been very subdued since Buchanan had lectured them. He wondered if they could shoot or if they would have the stamina to stand up under a siege.

Kovacs and his wife and Amanda were standing by a cleared long-table ready to reload guns as fast as they were emptied. All seemed calm enough. The Indian girl was again with Coco and Weevil, practicing her healing art. No one had shown panic at the first shots. They had been steeling themselves.

Durkin said, "I dunno, Buchanan. It don't look good to me."

"Now that's funny," Buchanan said. "I thought it looked just dandy."

"I ain't sure you know what you're doin'."

Buchanan found a mirror on the wall. He arranged it so that he could obtain a pretty good view of what was taking place outside the front of the house without exposing himself at the window.

He said to Durkin, "You want to try something? Make a run for the barn and help hold it down."

"I dunno if I want to. . . ."

Just then a white flag was waved from the woods. Without further ado, Durkin went to the back door and trailed his rifle out to the barn. Bradbury, Pollard, and Dealer Fox appeared, Pollard carrying the white cloth.

Buchanan called, "Not too close."

Pollard and Fox stopped, Bradbury walked on a few steps and shouted.

"Buchanan. Want to talk to you."

"Little late for that, Colonel."

"No. I don't want any unnecessary killin'."

"Just the necessary kind, huh? You with an army out there."

"Well, we want to get those people out of the country. Specially the women. They got to go, Buchanan. Ain't no two ways about it."

"Tell me more."

"They stole our cattle. They burnt Trevor out."

"Then why is it I am here?" Trevor called from the roof. "You liar."

"We'll make it up to you, Trevor. Build you a new house. Just you all surrender, and we'll make a deal. You leave the country. We pay the freight."

"I don't hear from Dealer or Morgan," Trevor retorted. "You're a fool, Brad. They've got you in a box."

"I'm backin' Brad," Fox said. "You can all take whatever you can tote and go. Nothin' will happen to you."

"Oh, what a story," said Rob Whelan. "Tell him to go straight to hell."

"Durkin," Fox yelled. "You're there some place. What about you?"

"Go to hell, like Whelan suggested," said Durkin from the barn. "I know you, and I know Morgan and Pollard."

"You people could start elsewhere," Bradbury urged. "There's plenty of places. Like I say, we'll pay you enough to get started again wherever you want to go."

"And keep our mouths shut forever," said Whelan. "Live out our lives with Adam Day hanged by the neck, us knowin' who done it."

"You see, these people don't want to be run off," Buchanan said. "They're right peculiar that way. You got one man down. How many do we have to send after him?"

"Too many," Pollard snarled. "C'mon, Boss." He tugged at Bradbury, who pulled himself away.

Buchanan said, "They got you, Colonel. They got you in a bind."

"The women." Bradbury was pleading now. "At least let the women go."

"You don't like that part?" Whelan was at the window now. "You dirty, lousy, lowdown skunk-bastards, you don't like it about the women? Well, lump it!"

Amanda Day said, "Let me, please." She went to stand beside Buchanan. He watched for movement on the knoll or in the trees, not trusting them for an instant.

She called, "The women decline. The women have seen your handiwork. They saw my husband. The whole town saw him. The women are staying."

Pollard said, "Y' see? C'mon."

Bradbury went unwillingly as his foreman hauled at him. Dealer Fox was already plodding back toward the trees. Buchanan was watching the top of the knoll. A man appeared, kneeling, his rifle pointed at the house.

There was a shot from the roof. The man tumbled and rolled down the hill. Shouts went up and a rataplan of lead rang from the stone house as bullets sought the sharpshooter. Trevor's laugh could be heard, light and merry.

"Could have been Dealer, y' know. Or better still, Pollard. Mind your manners, now. Who's next?"

The gunfire thundered, but no one showed himself. It was a good start, but a long day remained. And then there would be night.

Buchanan made the rounds, checking his forces. The open fields precluded an attack from the rear. The flanks were protected by the barn and the truck garden leading to the road. This was the only salvation he had been able to see.

He paused beside Kovacs. The man's face seemed thinner, his eyes were sunken, but he was unafraid. He had made his peace and was facing disaster as best he knew how.

Buchanan asked, "You got a handsaw around?"

"Saw?"

"That hole up yonder. If you could make it bigger I'd admire to make it to the roof. The sun and all, nobody can stay up there all day."

"Is so." He brightened. It was always good to have some definite task. He bustled into the kitchen.

Whelan was watching in Buchanan's mirror arrangement. "They'll be schemin' and augurin'. Bradbury, he's in bad, now."

"They won't rush us in the daytime." Buchanan made his voice light, confident for all to hear.

"If they got duck brains, they won't rush us nohow," said Fay Whelan.

"They got to," said Buchanan. "This house won't burn. They'll sharpshoot all day. Night comes, they got to move."

"Good thing we got the stable covered."

"If Durkin can hold it, that's a real hole card."

Fay asked, "You think he's on the level?"

"We'll watch the barn. Night and day."

If Durkin was a plant, the whole thing could go to pieces, Buchanan knew. He went into the kitchen. Amanda was preparing cold food that could be eaten quickly and easily. The Indian girl was stirring another brew on the stove, and Buchanan could detect a different odor to the herbs she was using.

"How is Weevil?" he asked her.

"Much better today."

"When can he handle a gun?"

"Soon." She looked at Buchanan. "It is the black man who hurts."

"Coco. His name is Coco. If it ever comes hand to hand, he'd be our best man."

"Yes. He is very strong." She indicated the pot on the stove. "There is much good here. These cures are handed down only by word of mouth, you know."

"I know. Your people are very wise."

She smiled gently. Her eyes were not quite black. They were wide-set and seemed to see more than the eyes of ordinary people. "You are a friend."

"Of the Crow, yes." He grinned at her. "I seen the time some Apaches and me didn't hit it off so good."

"I do not know Apaches. I know you do not tell lies."

"Not when the truth'll do," he told her.

"You are like Badger."

"Maybe a little, because we been around so long."

"The others, they are different," she whispered. "You must watch all of them excepting Pieter and Jenny."

"I'll watch. You do your best for Coco."

She nodded gravely, "I will do so."

The sound of Kovacs' saw was homey. It could have been reassuring if an occasional bullet had not winged its way to smash into a wall or a piece of furniture.

Amanda said, "I can't help ducking. As if it would do any good if one of them is meant for me."

"Only way to look at it," Buchanan told her.

"You're accustomed to fighting. It's just plain fortunate for us that you're here."

"Maybe." He need not boost the spirits of this woman, he felt. "A lot of luck's going to enter into this hooraw."

"I believe in you." She looked straight at him. "I wish we had met before. Any time before."

"It might've been real nice." He smiled at her. He had to remember that she had not been in love with her husband before he died. He wanted to respect her, there was something special about her.

"It would have been very nice indeed," she said.

He nodded and went out of the kitchen. Kovacs was coming down the ladder. A bullet slashed across the room and narrowly missed the saw. It caromed off the stone wall and went into the fireplace.

Kovacs said sadly, "Our house. We had pride in our house. We had love." He looked beyond Buchanan to where Raven was attending the two who had been battered. "Much love."

"I can see that." Buchanan felt more helpless every moment. No matter what the final result, there would be the damage to property, the certain injury to individuals. They all looked to him, and there was little he could do.

He climbed up to the roof with his rifle. He slid on elbows and knees to the parapet, thankful that the sharpshooters in the trees did not have the proper angle for a fair shot at him. As he crawled, he thought of the woman and the banked fires within her. For a long time, she endured her life with Adam Day with that fire slumbering. She must have been pushed to the limit to leave him—and she had been courageous to attempt to return, not for her own sake, but for Adam's.

The elder Thorne whined, "I'm mighty thirsty here in the sun."

"You're excused," said Buchanan. "Trevor, will you sorta take charge downstairs?"

"Right-o. Must say, Durkin's been takin' a few pot shots from the barn. Hasn't hit anything yet, though."

"Which could mean anything," said Buchanan.

"Shall watch," Trevor promised and followed Pa Thorne.

Sonny Thorne fingered an old rifle, squirmed, keeping his head down. "Mr. Buchanan?"

"Uh-huh."

" 'Bout the nigger."

"Black man, name of Coco Bean. Mister Bean to you."

"I seen buffalo sojers. Good men. Course, the blue uniform, that sets Pa off, us bein' Secesh."

"My father fought with Jackson."

"No foolin'?" The straw-haired thin man was surprised. "I woulda took you for a Yankee."

"Wasn't in it, myself. Took care of the home place."

"Well, wanted you to know. Pa, he goes on a lot. Can't say I'm altogether agin him. Ain't fer it, neither. Man's a man. Not that I'd want him to marry my sister."

"If you had a sister," Buchanan said, "Coco wouldn't want to marry her. Ever think of that?"

Sonny Thorne scowled for a moment. "Can't believe that. On t'other hand. I ain't got a sister." He brightened. "So best not to think on it."

"Uh-huh. Best not to strain yourself." Buchanan saw a movement in the trees and fired a shot. There was answering fire from the knoll, all directed at the roof. "Tryin' a sort of crossfire on us. Can't quite make it. They'll have to think of somethin' smart."

"If they was smart, they wouldn't've hung Adam," said Sonny Thorne with unexpected force. "Cause you know why?"

"Why?"

"Didn't nobody real care a damn for Adam. People liked her . . . Amanda. Adam was too muchety-much. He overdone it. He was honest and all. . . . But he rubbed it into people that didn't work as hard as he did, sunup to sundown. We ain't here on account of Adam Day."

"Then why are you here?"

"Them others, Bradbury and Fox and Crane, they pushed too hard. Pretty soon, we was in a corner." He grinned wryly. "You know how it is. Rats'll fight when cornered. And so will cats and just about everything else on earth."

Out of the mouths of the prejudiced ignorant, thought Buchanan, and out of the souls of people of every stage of life. There was no such thing as *little people* or *big people,* just human beings doing what had to be done. That fact made it easier for him to face impending disaster.

Colonel Bradbury sat on a fallen tree trunk and watched squat, ugly Toad Tanner drive a wagon into the clearing. There was a gunman on the seat with Tanner but none in the wagon body. Dealer Fox went to investigate. Bradbury wore his sixshooter for the first time in years and nursed a rifle upon his lap.

Fox asked, "You get the stuff okay?"

"Kegs of powder. All the dynamite in town." Tanner chuckled. "Wasn't easy. Store didn't want to sell out all his stock. People gettin' a bit techy in town."

"Hope you didn't start a ruckus."

"Naw. Just showed him my hawgleg and ast pretty. He come through."

"We don't want the town against us. Don't want them repairin' the telegraph line or makin' any noises. Got to be a mite careful there."

"Didn't hurt him none. Just sorta convinced him. Where you want the wagon?"

"Over back of the knoll, out of range of the house. Crane and Pollard'll tell you what to do."

Bradbury said nothing. Jigger Dorn was lounging nearby, grinning as always. There was never a moment one of them wasn't hanging around, watching.

It was getting to be a nightmare. The wagon contained enough explosives to blow up the countryside. And already there were two dead men buried over beyond the knoll. Drifters whose families would never know their last resting place. It had been easy to talk of subduing rustlers, fence-cutters, barn-burners. The doing of it was different. He had made his bid too late and, of course, had failed. They had been against it, they had sneered at him when it failed. Now he was virtually a prisoner.

"And if things go wrong, they'll find a way to kill me," he muttered to himself. Dorn was grinning at him. There was never any mirth in Dorn's grimace, he knew.

Tanner was saying, "Got to work to that stable. Mebbe tunnel underground, plant this here stuff. Ain't no other way agin that damn stone house."

"If we can set it afire, we can make a charge."

"They'd pick us off like settin' ducks," said Tanner. "Men ain't gonna just go and be shot down."

"They're bein' paid to fight. In advance. We got a heap of money invested here."

"Sure you do. And they figger to live to spend it." Tanner laughed. "Only thing you got goin' is the women. They'd like to git hold of them women."

Bradbury stirred. Tanner cast him a contemptuous glance. The wagon squeaked its way out of the glade. No one had bothered to grease the axles. There were too many men from different parts of the country and no one man to maintain strict order, which was a weakness. If he could get out of there, he thought, he might rid himself of complicity in the entire operation.

He said, "About the telegraph line, Dealer. Maybe I better take a couple men and make sure it stays down."

"Best idea you had yet," said Fox. He turned to Dorn. "Send three men to keep that wire down. Don't kill anybody. Just keep 'em away from where it's cut."

"Right," said Dorn.

Fox looked at Bradbury. "No way you can duck outa this, you know. We're in it together now."

A shaft of sunlight cut through the branches of the trees and fell upon the face of Bradbury's longtime neighbor and associate. "Why, Dealer, you're scared! You're as scared as I am!"

Fox ducked his head into shade. "Maybe I am. Maybe this won't go like it should. But by God, I'm stickin'. I ain't runnin' out like an old woman."

"Stickin'," said Bradbury. "I suppose that makes you a man."

"It makes out that we got everything at stake here, and

I don't give a damn who suffers, I'm savin' my own skin."

Bradbury nodded. "Yes. Lookin' back, I see it. You was always out to save your hide. All the way through. You and that fool Morgan Crane. He thinks you're real clever. Maybe you are, Dealer, maybe you are. But this time, you and Morgan bit off a big chaw."

Fox turned abruptly away. He walked to where the old killer, Dab Geer, sat honing a Bowie knife. He motioned toward Bradbury with his head, and Geer showed toothless gums in a leer. It was better to talk with Morgan and Pollard at this time. They had no trepidation, they knew the stone house could be destroyed with all who were inside.

Bradbury debated with himself. He could shoot Geer with the rifle from where he sat. He could get to his horse and make a run for it. He might even be able to send a message to the governor asking help, thus removing himself from the siege and all that it stood for.

But he could not bring Adam Day back to life. The town knew. Pollard had been at the lynching, and Pollard was Bradbury's man. The parade of the corpse through the town had labeled him. The fight with Buchanan—everyone knew what was involved. Trevor's abdication, the burning of Trevor's place, a stupid operation now that he thought about it. Nobody believed the story about Trevor and Fay Whelan. Only fools would think up such nonsense to make a case for themselves.

Dealer was right. They were in it together. They were in *for* it in every manner and fashion. The only way out was to destroy the witnesses and hope the word of the Cattleman's Association and their hired guns would prevail.

If he had only thought it through beforehand, if Buchanan had only arrived earlier, before the lynching . . . His mind boggled. He sat staring at the gun in his hands, an aging man lost in his own land.

On the lee side of the knoll, Dealer Fox spoke privately to Morgan Crane. "Supposin' somebody does repair the telegraph wire before our men can get to it?"

"Dammit to hell, why didn't we leave a guard on it?"

"We didn't. So we got to move fast. We got to get to that barn, then to the house."

"Yeah. You're right, Dealer. Blow up the damn place." Morgan Crane stared down the lee side of the small hill. "How we goin' to do that? There's too much open space yonder twixt us and the barn."

"Sime," called Dealer Fox. "Sime!"

The foreman of Bar-B strolled up from the wagon, a seamy-faced man, a veteran of the cattle drives, the honky-tonks, the gambling dens. "Got enough ammunition, all right. Now what is it?"

"The barn," Crane said in his harsh manner. "Gotta get the dynamite and stuff down there and blow 'em out."

Pollard looked at Fox. "He gone crazy or somethin'?"

"It's got to be done and quick."

"You're gettin' the wind up," Pollard said. "Slow down. They got us stopped for a while."

Fox said, "The telegraph wire. Somebody could send for troops, militia."

Pollard shrugged. "That's your business. There's nobody here would try and get to that stable in daytime. And I ain't too sure about night."

Fox bit at a fingernail. "All right. Night. We'll try it after dark."

"We? You goin' down there?" Pollard grinned.

"I'll damn well go," yelled Crane. "What's got into you, Sime? How come you're speakin' up so biggety?"

"My neck's on the line," Pollard told him. "Half the men we got here came on account of I sent for 'em. They ain't makin' any brash moves without me okayin' 'em. See?"

Fox said hastily, "We appreciate, Sime. We know what you done . . . are doin'. But we got to move fast."

Pollard said, "I'll think on it." He went back to the wagon, speaking to the men, ordering the safe storage of the explosives and the boxes of ammunition, not looking back at the ranchmen.

Crane growled, "Brad never could handle him. Spiled him rotten. He needs to be took down a peg or two."

"Brad's already been taken down," mused Fox. "He won't ever be the same man."

"The others don't count," said Crane. "They ain't here, they won't mean nothin' when this is over."

"Right." The other members of the association had not been consulted. They would not interfere, but neither would they take part in the siege, Fox knew. They were spread far and wide over Wyoming and southern Montana and would leave everything to Bradbury, Fox, and Crane, providing only the funds from the common treasury and silent support. It could be an opportunity to move into a commanding position in the cattle business of two states. "Morgan?"

"Yeah?"

"If Brad and Sime don't come outa this alive that makes us boss. Right?"

"Brad won't show himself to get kilt. Pollard? I dunno."

"Sime's got all those gunners with him. Might be a good idea to take care of him afore he tries somethin' on his own."

Crane considered. "Dorn's my man. Maybe Tanner and Geer, too. They got a few will stick."

Fox nodded. "First we blow up them damn rustlers and such. Then we take care of Brad and Sime."

"Take care of 'em?" Crane was always slow.

"One way or another. They're dangerous."

"Dangerous? Yeah . . . well, okay."

Fox was staring at the wagon. He said, "I got it."

"Yeah?" Crane's mind could never quite keep up.

"The wagon. Come dark, they can use it for cover. Wheel it down to the barn. See how that could work?"

"Hey, you always do think up somethin' good. Lemme go tell Sime."

"No," said Fox. "Not now. Wait."

"Why wait, Dealer?"

"Let Pollard stew a bit. Then we'll spring it on him."

"If you say so. I'm gonna send a few more rounds through them windows. Might get somebody lucky. Wish I could get at that Trevor. Or Buchanan."

"Maybe you will, Morgan. Maybe you will." He

watched the big man go for his rifle. Maybe it would be a good idea if Trevor or Buchanan got Crane, he thought. Then there would only be one supreme outfit in the country. People were so damn stupid, they got in a man's way. . . .

They had been his friends, but in his life, he had found that friendship could be costly.

Buchanan was on the roof. He had an old-fashioned spyglass that Jenny Kovacs had produced, saying, "Vas my father's." There was no action near any tree that could command high gun against the house. Trevor, then the Whelans, and now Buchanan had been able to sweep that section and keep it clear.

The firing from the barn had been sporadic. The wide doors at each end were parallel to the zone of enemy fire, and Durkin's men had to be wary of showing themselves. There was no way that Buchanan could yet be certain of Durkin. Only time would tell about his true loyalty. He had his own food and guns and ammunition—and his own notions.

There were hollow, ringing sounds from below, then a cry of pain. Trevor came onto the roof, crawling to Buchanan.

"The elder Thorne," he said. "Add one to the wounded."

"I've been thinking about that," said Buchanan. He handed the spyglass to Trevor. "I'll send the Whelans up. This is the best possible place long as there's light to aim by."

"Right-o."

Buchanan went below. The Indian girl was already attending to Pa Thorne, who had been hit in the chest by a ricochet. The wound seemed serious enough and Buchanan went into action. He removed the mattress from a bed and figured angles, then hung it on the wall.

He said, "Get everything that'll prevent a bullet from bouncin' around. Rugs, pillows, everything. Look at where they been hittin', cover that spot. Sorry about your belongin's, Jenny, Pieter."

"Is nothing." But their eyes proved they were not telling

the whole truth. They had built and furnished a house of which they were proud, and now it was being ripped apart.

Raven called, "I think you had better come, Mr. Buchanan."

Pa Thorne was stretched on the long table. He was breathing with difficulty. A lung had been punctured, Buchanan knew at once. The pale eyes were losing what little light had been in them.

Thorne whispered, "What you said about the nigra. I thought on it. I don't want to go with my evil beliefs on my conscience."

"Well, then, you don't have to worry," Buchanan told him. "You made it up, thinkin' on it."

The dying man looked at his son. "See? I ain't got no bad feelin's no more. It's all right. You fight 'em, Sonny."

"You'll be all right, Pa. Don't talk like that."

"Never did have much good lungs," said Pa Thorne. He coughed once, then closed his eyes. Raven shook her head, touching him.

"He's gone," said Buchanan. He picked up the body, wrapping the blanket about it. He carried it into the corner of the second bedroom and deposited it there. It was another problem, corpses could not be stacked like logs, there had to be a disposition of them. He found Sonny Thorne behind him, dry-eyed but solemn.

"Comes night, we'll bury him," Buchanan said.

"Yes. Y' know, I'm wonderin'. Pa and the way we live. Raisin' hawgs, gettin' drunk in town, seein' the whores. 'Tain't much of a life."

"It's what you and him were fightin' for," Buchanan said.

"Y' know, the association never even made us an offer."

"They didn't have to, Sonny."

"I know, you're plumb right. They'd just gobble us up." His knuckles tightened on the old rifle he had not relinquished. "They got Pa, all right. But by God, they ain't got me yet. I aim to git me a couple of 'em afore they do."

He went to a window and stared out. A bullet whizzed past his head and struck one of the cloth mufflers the Ko-

vacs and Amanda had hung. Sonny poked out the gun and
returned the fire, wildly, just to serve notice.

Buchanan went across to where Coco was sitting up in
bed. "You feelin' more like yourself?"

"That lil ole Injun gal," Coco said wonderingly. "She is
pure voodoo."

"Not voodoo. Crow Indian. They know a lot of things."

"Prettiest lil ole gal I ever did see." Coco was not usually interested in females; he was a dedicated prizefighter,
always in top condition in case a bout should be proferred.
When the urge became too strong, he had always been
able to find a house that obliged with a convenient black
woman. "Her hands are like the wings of doves."

"Doves?" Buchanan stared. "Like doves?"

"You just don't understand. You just a big bullyboy.
That gal's healin' me. It's a plain miracle."

"I'M a big bullyboy? YOU are a little flower? I swan,
Coco, you must still be possessed by the fever."

"Go tend to your fightin'," said Coco. "I get up outa
here, I'm goin' to whup you all over Wyomin'."

"That's better," said Buchanan. He looked at Weevil.
"What about you?"

"Had the dizzys. They whomped me so on the head that
my eyes got crossed. Like Coco says, the gal knows what
to do. Gimme a gun anytime you're ready. I can do any-
thin' but scout. A one-legged scout won't cut it."

Buchanan nodded. It was time to check with Durkin in
the barn. He went into the kitchen. Amanda was again
putting together sandwiches.

"Food holdin' out?" he asked her.

"Everybody brought some. But there are a lot of
mouths to feed. Have some soup."

It was best to eat when he could get it, there would
come a time when he'd miss meals, he knew. She paused
to watch him, smiling secretly. He was uneasy.

"It ain't funny. One of us gone already," he said.

"I know. You make it plain." Still she smiled at the
corners of her mouth, with her eyes. "You do go all the
way. You don't mince words."

"Wouldn't be right to cheat people with promises. In this

kind of a fight, everybody should feel like he or she won't get it. Correct. But you can't get around the odds."

"We face the odds every day of our lives," she told him. "I'm thinking of the time when this is over."

"That's good."

"Of you and me. We'll be . . . friends."

Again he noted how each varying emotion transfigured her, made her interesting, even beautiful. "Sure. We'll be friends. If we live."

Raven came into the kitchen and accepted soup. He had yet to see her really smile. She moved always to where she was most needed, silent, graceful. He could imagine how Coco felt about her.

She said, "Your fighting man is afraid of guns, isn't he?"

"He tell you that?"

"He spoke of many things he will not remember."

"Yeah, the fever. But he does hate guns. Scared? No. I never knew Coco to be scared."

"A fine man," she said, stating it as a fact.

"You oughta hear what he says about you."

"I have heard." Now she did smile slightly, her eyes widening. "It is nice to know what a man feels."

"You'll know a heap about men before you're through," he told her, grinning.

She sobered immediately, lowering her eyes to the soup. He had met nuns like her, he thought, dedicated to others, selfless.

He finished the soup and went to the back door. The sun still shone as it dipped toward the mountains. Clouds billowed in the sky. The open door of the barn seemed a mile away. The sharpshooters in the trees and on the knoll were watching. Every so often they would fire a shot on the chance of hitting someone.

Buchanan hitched up his pants. Without warning, he opened the door and began to run toward the stable. He heard Amanda gasp, "No!" behind him. He zigged and zagged. He could cover ground like a grizzly, with deceptive speed.

Bits of lead tore the ground before him and behind him.

In another moment, they would have the range. He made a last great leap, and as a bullet zipped past his head, he gained the door of the barn.

Durkin said in his hard voice, "Well, you made it. What you got in your head?"

"How do you feel about it?"

Durkin thrust out his prominent jaw. "You gonna come out here with me?"

Buchanan thought a moment. "Uh-huh. You two come into the house when the light fails. Durkin and me, we'll see how it goes. There'll be people on the roof of the house. That suit you?"

Durkin looked at the cowboys. "You heard him."

"Yeah. And you ain't got a ghost of a chance if they make a rush," said Cactus.

"And if we ain't—then you'll be in a hell of a fix when they take the barn," said Buchanan.

"Six of one, half a dozen of the other," Durkin remarked. "Thing is, I wouldn't have a chance nohow unless we stop 'em right here. Them people in there, they ain't my kind. I'm lookin' out for me. I ain't no hero."

"Most heroes are dead," said Buchanan.

"I noticed."

"I'll be goin' in now. You want to cover me?"

Durkin said, "Not particular. I ain't so crazy about you neither, y' know."

"I figured."

"But every gun counts, and you got them people buffaloed into believin' you're the second comin'. So git goin'." Durkin took his rifle and went to the door at the west end of the barn. The cowboys hesitated, then joined him.

Buchanan began to run. There were shots that came too close. He flung himself down on the ground and rolled for the cover of the corral.

The three guns from the barn began to speak in unison. Buchanan did not wait to learn the results. He jumped up and continued on his way pell mell. Amanda held the door open, and he dove into the kitchen, sliding with his head under the table.

Amanda slammed the door and knelt beside him. "Are you hurt? Did they get you?"

"Might's well. Scared me to death." Buchanan sat up. "You sure do look pretty when you get exercised."

She flushed and stood up, moving toward the stove. "We couldn't do without you, now, could we?"

"You might not do too good with me," he told her.

The sun was going down. Buchanan went into the other room and made his announcement, two more guns in the house, Trevor and the Whelans on the roof because they could be trusted.

"Coco, Weevil, you keep your eyes on Cactus and Sutter. They make a wrong move, you, Weevil, you shoot 'em. Coco won't do it, and he ain't able to scrag 'em."

"You still don't trust them?" asked Trevor.

"Nope. Could be Durkin wants to get me, figurin' them to take over the house."

"Then why not put them on the roof with us?"

"You'll be too busy to watch 'em close enough." He looked at Weevil. "You seein' straight now?"

"Fine, thankee." He picked a revolver from the armament on the long table. "Up close I can get 'em both. I think."

Kovacs said quietly, "I watch. If I got to, I get one."

"Good."

"I do not like," Kovacs said. "But I do it."

"Nobody likes any of this," Buchanan told him. "Prob'ly some people out yonder don't like it, neither."

But Kovacs was unhappy, he knew. The man had not complained, but it had to be a fearful time for him, his wife, and their adopted Indian girl. Amanda seemed tougher, more dedicated. The Whelans knew what had to be done and would carry through. Trevor was somewhat detached but willing.

The problem was that they all looked to Buchanan, who had no stake in the fight—all excepting Durkin, perhaps. Someone had to outmaneuver the enemy, and none but Buchanan had the experience and the quality of leadership.

Except, perhaps, Durkin again. He went to the door and set himself for the short run. He called to the people on the roof, and they laid down a line of fire.

He made the quick dash. This time only two shots came close, but either one would have killed him. He wondered if his luck was gradually running short.

Durkin greeted him. "Looks like rain. You fix things up with them in the house?"

"Anytime your boys want to try and make it."

Durkin said to the cowboys, "You seen Buchanan do it. Make up your minds."

They hesitated, looking at one another. Then Cactus went to the door. Buchanan joined Durkin. Trevor waved from the rooftop, and they began to fire. Cactus darted toward the house where Amanda held the door open. He made it.

Sutter said, "Well, here goes nothin'."

He lowered his head and went in a bull rush. He was a heavy man and lacked speed, agility.

He was almost to the house when he went down, one leg knocked from under him. Buchanan, watching even as he fired at the sharpshooters on the knoll, saw him fall.

He said, "Keep at it, Durkin," and ran.

He made his zigzag pattern. As he came close to Sutter, the bullets were raining about him. Without breaking stride, he picked up the heavy man and hurled him through the open door, following, dragging Sutter past Amanda. The door slammed and Amanda's white face betrayed her fear.

Raven came. They stretched Sutter on the table. The bullet had gone cleanly through the calf of his leg. The Indian girl went to work on it as though she had been trained in a first-class hospital.

Sutter looked up at Buchanan. "Much obliged. They woulda filled me with lead if you hadn't come along."

Cactus said, "Never did see a man so damn strong. Sutter, he ain't no lightweight."

"Just you two help these people in here," Buchanan said. "Just try and make a fight."

Sutter winced, then grinned. "Thought we might cross yawl, didn'tcha, Buchanan?"

"It ran through my mind."

"Ran through ours, too. Like they might've paid us off big if we pulled it out for 'em."

Buchanan said, "You wouldn't have got away with it. So don't do us any favors. Just be good boys."

He took a deep breath. He looked at the barn door. It seemed as though it had moved farther away from the house. Twilight was coming on, and he could wait and diminish the risk. But Durkin was out there alone. It was wrong to leave a man to himself at a time like this.

Buchanan ran. Again they came close to hitting him. He did not know if it was closer than before, but he could not shake off the feeling that sooner or later one of those bullets would bear his name.

Durkin was staring out through the gathering darkness toward the enemy on the knoll. They would furnish the problem of the coming night. The sharpshooters in the trees would not attack lest they be cut down in the clearing in front of the house.

Buchanan said, "Sutter got it in the leg, nice and clean."

"Hadda happen. Thought they might get you this time."

"Uh-huh," said Buchanan. "Had the same thought myself."

"Yuh never know," said Durkin. He glanced at Buchanan. "Mighty white of you, pickin' up Sutter. You don't even know him or nothin'."

"Seems like a good enough man."

"Just about," said Durkin. " 'Twas a big thing to do. I ain't forgettin' it."

They settled down to wait. As always, waiting was the worst of it.

7

Now it began to rain, a steady, dismal drizzle. Buchanan stared at the knoll; he sensed there was much activity back there. There had been little firing from that direction in the last hour.

No light shone from the house, lest the inhabitants be lined as targets for the men in the trees. Once in a while, there was a flash of lightning and Trevor and the Whelans tried to pick off those across from them with little success.

Durkin said, "Buchanan, you mind when we first butted heads?"

"A long while ago. East Texas," said Buchanan.

"We was youngsters. There was that Fourth of July turkey shoot and fair."

"I remember." He wondered what they could be up to out of his sight and sound, behind that hill.

"I was bigger'n you, then. There was a little gal named Susie Brown. I was courtin' her."

"That I don't remember."

"You won the turkey. You won the sack race. You won the potato race. Then we rassled."

"Uh-huh. I remember that. You were strong as an ox."

"Yeah. And you throwed me."

"A trick," said Buchanan. "Pa taught me."

"Susie Brown, she went home with you."

"She did, now?" He thought he heard harness creaking. He wished Durkin would stop reminiscing.

"Never would go with me no more. From that day, I swore to get to be a bigger and better man than you, Buchanan. I worked. I saved. Lost it all a couple times. Oh, I heard about you. Ran across you in El Paso that time. Seems to me you didn't have nothin'. I was gatherin' some beef, then."

"That's right. You were doin' right good." A wagon wheel squealed beyond the knoll.

"You moved up and down and around. You ain't got a thing except what you carry on you. Right?"

"Yep," said Buchanan. "That's correct."

"I got land. Paid for. I got cattle grazin' that land. I got a nice house and am lookin' for a bride."

"That's right fine." Now there were voices, but he could not distinguish a word that was said.

"Yep. I finally had things goin' good. Then this happened. Never would knuckle down, you know that. Bound to prove I'm a better man than you."

Buchanan couldn't see the man's face, but the seriousness of his mien was patent in his voice. "Why, that's okay with me. I like what I do. I hope you live to own Wyoming, Durkin."

"And here you come. Ready to fight. Nothin' to gain. Just a damn hero."

"Nope," said Buchanan. "Scared. And hooked into it without meanin' to take a hand."

"Yeah? Well, when this is over you are goin' to answer to me, Buchanan. We'll see who's the best man."

"You'll have to get in line," Buchanan said. "Coco's first."

There was more noise behind that knoll. He was certain he detected the reflected light of torches. He had to know what was going on. Again a wagon wheel creaked.

"I dunno what you're talkin' about. But we'll see who's who." Durkin was becoming agitated by his long-standing grievance. His voice grew louder, he swung his long, heavy arms. "You hear me? You're gonna have to show me. This time I'm gonna beat out what little brains you got."

He peered into the darkness. The rain fell gently on the roof of the barn. He reached out a hand.

"Buchanan?"

There was no reply. He whirled around.

"You hidin' on me?"

Still no answer. Suddenly Durkin felt alone. He dared not strike a taper and make himself a target. He swung around the barn, calling Buchanan's name. It took him a few moments to realize what had happened. He shook himself together, bringing his mind to the present.

He listened. He looked. He cursed beneath his breath. Then he levered a shell into the chamber of his rifle and rolled out of the barn, a squat, heavy man prowling into blackness, feeling the rain on his face, going in a circle, approaching the scene of activity behind the little hill.

Buchanan was already out there. He was in the open, and if a sudden wind should come up and dispel the clouds, he would be in a very unpleasant position indeed. At least he didn't have to listen to Durkin, he thought, applying all his plainsmanship to sneaking around the northern tip of the knoll. He stopped and listened again. Wagon springs creaked as though someone was loading up. He was getting closer to the enemy ranks. He heard Morgan Crane's loud voice, and a man laughed, and he thought that was Jigger Dorn. He flattened himself and crawled on wet grass.

Then he saw the torches planted in the ground. There was the wagon with the squeaky wheel. It was almost to the top of the knoll, and it was headed for the barn. There were men behind it, but no horses to pull it.

Dealer Fox was giving orders. Pollard was talking to men who now aligned themselves on the side of the wagon that would not be exposed to fire from the house or the barn.

There was a steady fire from the trees at the front of the house now. It was a much steadier attack than before.

Morgan Crane yelled, "Make sure you get the damn fuses lit in time."

"Yeah," Buchanan breathed. "Thank goodness for one big mouth tonight, anyway."

They were getting ready, he saw. He moved with speed down into the path the wagon must take to get to the barn. Now he wished he had brought out Trevor or the Whelans to help. Durkin might do some good from the barn. . . .

A shot sounded. One of the men at the wagon went down. There was a shout. The wagon began to move, propelled by the men behind it and alongside it. It picked up speed going down the hill.

Durkin's powerful voice echoed in the night, "Buchanan! Where the hell are you? They're gonna blow up the damn barn!"

Twenty men behind the hill turned guns toward the sound of the voice. Buchanan lay flat and began firing as swiftly as he could pull the trigger.

There could be no help from the house. They were out of that line of fire. Durkin still shot into the mass of the enemy. Men fell, there was confusion . . . but the wagon was rolling rapidly, and now Buchanan saw the glow of the tip of a fuse.

He emptied the rifle. Then he began to run. Durkin was still shooting. Men scrambled away from the wagon. They had lashed the front axle so that it would remain on course. He stumbled over a prone body, recovered himself. As he twisted around, he caught a glimpse of Durkin, who had rushed into the light of the torches.

The underslung rancher had his revolver in his hand.

He was fanning it, not bothering to aim. The attention of the entire crew was on him.

They fired at him. He went down on one knee. He reached behind his neck and yanked out a long, gleaming Bowie knife. He rushed at them.

Buchanan gulped. He was at the tailgate of the wagon. He tossed the rifle aboard. He grabbed hold with both hands and vaulted into the body of the wagon.

He had to go by the feel of things, now. He saw the spark of the fuse. It led to a box, upon which was stacked another box. There was enough dynamite to blow up half the county. The rain had stopped, but everything was slippery and greasy. He scrabbled with his hands.

All the men had fallen or been shot away from the wagon. Buchanan stumbled and fell as the speed decreased. There was just enough momentum to reach the barn. They had timed it well.

One hand touched the fuse. He snuffed it out. He clambered at once to the seat of the wagon. There was still danger that it would collide with the stone barn, that a spark would set off the whole thing.

He reached for the wagon pole, which had been lashed to keep the axle from swerving. He took it in his hands and braced his feet, swinging out with all his might.

He felt something give. The front wheels spun loose. He came down on the pole. His muscles swelled to bursting under the strain.

He pointed the wagon north and slightly away from the barn. He exerted the last remnant of his enormous power. Inch by inch, he fought the wagon to a standstill. Leaning hard against it, he sagged against the pole for a moment, drawing deep breath into his aching lungs.

Durkin had proved himself, he thought now. Durkin had died proving to himself that he was the better man. It was good that he believed that, going down and out. Certainly he had given Buchanan time and opportunity to act. If dying well proved anything, Durkin must have been satisfied with his end.

Shots were coming at the wagon. Buchanan found strength to climb into the body. There were kegs, obvious-

ly containing gunpowder. He moved these and the boxes
of dynamite to the rear end of the wagon body.

He heard voices from the barn, then. Kovacs called to
him, and then Cactus yelled for Durkin.

Buchanan said, "Here."

They came running. They stared at the wagon. The
clouds were drifting away, there was starlight.

Buchanan said, "Cactus, cover us. Pieter, help me get
this stuff into the barn before we all get blown to bits."

"Where's Durkin?" Cactus was already lining up the
men showing themselves on the knoll.

Buchanan handed a heavy keg of powder to Kovacs,
who ducked his head as he lugged it into the barn. " 'Fraid
he went over. He was tryin' to stop 'em."

Cactus began to shoot. Buchanan picked up a box of
dynamite and, carrying it as though it were a crate of eggs,
ran past Kovacs into the shelter of the stone stable. Kovacs was scared as bullets came wildly out of the night, but
he too brought in a box of dynamite.

Cactus said, "He was a hard man, Durkin. But fair."

"He went out dead game," Buchanan told him. It
seemed the second keg of powder was heavier than the
first. He staggered with Kovacs into the barn. He remembered his rifle and jumped into the wagon to retrieve it. A
bullet whistled past his ear. He juggled the rifle, knelt, inserted cartridges. He leveled at the knoll and sent shot
after shot at the exposed enemy.

Out of the distant darkness, now dimly lit by the stars,
came a booming sound. Morgan Crane bellowed something and the firing toward the barn ceased.

"What the hell was that?" demanded Cactus, reloading.

"That was Dan Badger," Buchanan told him, sighing in
relief. "What you heard was a Sharps buffalo gun. Makes
people stop and think."

"They will catch him," said Kovacs fearfully. "They
will kill my friend."

"I doubt it," said Buchanan. "Let's get this junk stored
where it can do the most good."

Cactus said, "This stuff could blow us all to hell."

"Is so," said Kovacs.

"The powder's no good to us, maybe. But the dynamite might be useful," Buchanan said.

"No!" Kovacs was white but determined. "Is blow up my house, everyt'ing. No!"

Buchanan felt the strong opposition. He asked, "What do you think we're goin' to do with it? Eat it?"

The shooting from the trees slowed down. Clouds drifted back to blot out the stars. It did not rain, but it was a black night.

Kovacs said, "Off my property. I will take it away. Out there." He pointed to the back of the house and the open fields.

"Where it can be set off by a bolt of lightning, any spark?"

"Is then God decides." Kovacs crossed himself. "Is not to blow up my house. My barn."

"The Lord helps them as helps themselves," Buchanan said. "I say we cover this stuff up, protect it, and maybe it will save us all."

Cactus asked, "Who's goin' to stay out here and watch over it? Not me, Buchanan. You already got my boss killed. I ain't lookin' for any of the same."

"Uh-huh." In the darkness, Buchanan composed himself. It was the time to be patient. He had seen Kovacs bend under the strain earlier in the day. As the siege continued, the pressure would be greater on them all. "Tell you what. You do what you want with the powder."

Before they could detect what he was up to, he picked up a box of dynamite under each arm. "I'll put this where it won't do any harm to us."

"No!" cried Kovacs. He ran at Buchanan, missed him in the dark, fell into a stall on his face.

Buchanan kept on going. When he got to the back door, Amanda was there, waiting, holding it open for him.

"What happened?" she asked breathlessly.

"Plenty," Buchanan told her. "Which is the closet with the most room?"

She led the way to the door. He put the boxes down with great care. "Bring me a lantern, please."

The others were crowding around now. He motioned

them back. Amanda came, shielding the light so that it would not betray them to the gunners across the way.

Buchanan stowed the two boxes of dynamite in the depths of the closet. Nothing less than a cannon ball could break through the stone walls, he thought. It was as safe as a silver dollar.

He got out his Barlow and pried open one of the boxes. The sticks were packed in sawdust with care. He needed now only to get back to the wagon and find caps and a couple of coils of fuse.

He sat back on his haunches and looked at Amanda. For once in his strenuous existence, he was thoroughly weary. His exertions of the past hour had been prodigious. Worse, they had not quite been appreciated by at least two of the company of defenders.

She said softly, "You should get some rest."

"Can't make it right now," he told her. He got to his feet and stretched. "Kovacs is crackin'. How about the others?"

"Why . . . everything seems as it was," she said. "There were almost no ricochets, thanks to your buffers. Trevor and the Whelans are on the roof."

"Yes, I know. They did good." He hated to send them to the barn. It was the most vulnerable spot. He went to the rear door, paused. "Try and talk to Jenny. I got to see what I can do outdoors right now."

The Indian girl drifted to his side. "Let me speak with Pieter."

"That might work." He hesitated, but the girl was past him and running before he could stop her. He followed.

It was still dark in the barn. Cactus was standing near the door closest to the house. As if she could see in the night, Raven swerved and sped into the field behind the barn.

Cactus said, "He took the powder out there."

"He's got the wind up," said Buchanan. "Can't hold it against him. He's never been in this fix before."

"Ain't likely to be in one again," said the cowboy. "This here'll be the last if somethin' ain't done."

"Something like what?"

"There's horses out there, I heard 'em. Best we should round 'em up and ride out before mornin'."

"You think the women could get away?"

"Some of us could. Way it is, nobody's got a chance."

"Bradbury offered to let us go."

"That was before Durkin got his'n. Things is different now, leastways for me. Sutter too, I expect."

"Sutter's in no shape to ride. But if you want to go, Cactus, grab yourself a saddle and dab a pony. Nobody's holdin' you here."

He could not see the man, but he could almost feel the thought processes going on. Finally, Cactus said slowly, "I mind the man left the Alamo. He lived. But it was a bad life. No, I ain't about to go alone. I'll stick. For now."

Buchanan said, "Okay. Now, there's a dead man in the house. Supposin' you go in there and tote him out here and tuck him in a corner of the barn. It's no good leavin' corpses around live folks. Makes 'em think too much of what might happen."

"Who, me? I ain't no undertaker."

Buchanan said, "Cactus."

"Yeah?"

"Either go in there and tote out old Thorne, or get that rope and saddle and ride out."

After a moment, the cowboy said, "Okay. But I ain't forgettin' any of this. I'll see you later, maybe."

"Uh-huh," said Buchanan wearily. "You do that."

Poor Durkin had not lived to carry out the threat. Maybe this one would. Someone was always coming after him with intent to do bodily harm. It was a sorry circumstance, especially for a peaceable man.

He waited at the barn door, but there were no shots coming from the knoll. He thought that Badger's long rifle may have caused them to hole up, count their losses, and think awhile. He climbed into the wagon again.

He found the fuse, a good-sized coil. There were several caps scattered about the wooden bottom of the wagon body. He picked them up. He was able to find only a half dozen. He wished there were a dozen more. He put them in his pocket and dropped back to earth.

Badger's big gun boomed again. The old mountain man was keeping them occupied all right. Buchanan went into the barn.

The Indian girl called, "Mr. Buchanan."

"Uh-huh."

She came close to him. "He has put the powder far from the house. It is hard to talk to him. He is disturbed."

"Yeah, I know how it is for him."

"I think there will be more trouble."

Buchanan said, "Lordy me, gal, you're right. You don't know how right you are."

"Dan Badger is out there. I could go to him."

"Reckon you could. You do get around. But we need you here real bad. Who'd take care of the wounded?"

"Yes. You are right." She was silent. "I will wait until I have spoken with Dan Badger."

"If he comes in, you mean?"

"He will come in when he is needed," she said. She had complete confidence. "You will see."

"I'll be happy to see."

They went back into the house. It was still pitch dark. Amanda had fixed the lantern so that it shed light only for a few feet around it, placing it behind the door. Kovacs sat on a kitchen chair, staring at nothing. His wife sat beside him, her hand on his arm. They were silent. Raven went to them, but they did not move or speak.

Buchanan went up to the roof. He had to drag himself, he was so weary. Trevor and the Whelans were stretched out on blankets. An occasional shot came from the trees, and once in a while, they answered in order to let the attackers know the house was well defended.

Buchanan said, "Someone's goin' to have to take over in the barn."

"How come?" asked Rob Whelan.

He told them about Durkin, about the brief mutiny, about the breakdown of the Kovacs. They listened, and he could feel the dampening of their spirits. He ended, "Maybe the Whelans, huh? I know you want to be together. The two of you could do the job. I'll be movin' back and forth."

"You believe they will try the barn again?" Trevor asked.

"They may make a charge in the dark. They may make it any minute. But we got the best of that. The barn's their best bet."

Fay Whelan said, "Durkin wouldn't have got it if he hadn't gone out."

"Maybe not."

"What do you say, Rob?"

"I say there's straw to bed down in. We can take turns watchin'. It's risky all right, But what ain't?"

Buchanan said, "I'll stay up here for a while."

"Any orders for down below?" asked Rob Whelan.

"It ain't the time to be givin' orders. Like I said, we got some problems," Buchanan said. "You want to swap blankets? You take mine to the stable, leave yours here?"

"Why . . . sure."

"I'll be checkin' with you later."

They went down from the roof. Buchanan rolled onto the blankets.

Trevor asked, "Is there anything I can do, old man?"

"Old man is right," said Buchanan. "Just . . . watch . . . awhile . . . wake me before sunup. . . ." His head dropped. He was asleep.

Colonel Bradbury fought against sleep. In the glade, there was a meeting of furious, red-eyed, cursing men. Over behind the knoll, the sound of shovels could be heard. They were digging a trench to bury the dead. The wounded lay in the trees on the damp earth and bled. The odor of moss collided with the odor of their blood.

Bradbury had been a sergeant in the Big War. The title of Colonel was self-administered when he came to Texas long ago; it lent dignity. For that matter, hundreds of others had done the same. But he did know the rudiments of military action, and he knew the sickness that came upon many men in battle. He was afraid to sleep.

It would be easy for them to dispose of him, now that the fever was on them. They could throw him in the trench and tell any sort of lie to cover themselves. There were so many of them now that confusion reigned.

Fox was saying, "We got to run over 'em. The wagon full of dynamite was a good notion, but that goddam Buchanan and that fool Durkin spoiled it."

"We got Durkin," said Morgan Crane. "I been wantin' him outa the way."

"We just got to go down there and blast 'em out. There's more dynamite," Fox insisted.

"They ain't up to it," Pollard said. "Too many of 'em caught it with the wagon."

"We're payin' them plenty."

"That makes no never mind," Pollard told him. "Gunnies want a chance to live, too. You got to reckon on that Buchanan."

"It was Brad sent for him." Fox stared at his friend and ally.

Bradbury spoke. "It was some of you hung Adam Day. That's what turned Buchanan. I know him."

"Then you shouldn't have sent for him."

Bradbury shrugged. He was in a hopeless position.

Pollard said, "I'm beginnin' to feel like I know him good. And lemme tell you, what I know I don't like for a damn."

"We'll get him and all the rest," roared Crane. "Dealer's right. We got the men. We can run right over that little bunch of nothin' down there."

"I still say we get to the barn," said Fox. "One way or another. Dig under the house and blow 'em to hell."

"Who's goin' to dig?" asked Pollard.

"Get the barn and someone'll dig. I'll put a gun on 'em if I have to," Crane said.

"You think Buchanan wouldn't know what was goin' on?"

"What could he do about it?"

"Set a counter-charge," Bradbury told them.

"There's got to be some way." Fox was beside himself. "All these guns, everything we got."

"That there house is like a fort," said Bradbury. "You

lay a siege, starve 'em out. Pick off whoever shows himself. It takes time. And we've not got that much time."

"The boss is right," said Pollard. "We got Durkin, maybe we got a couple more through the windows. We got to keep pastin' them thataway."

"Word is bound to get out. There'll be trouble . . . maybe the militia, maybe even the damn army."

"That's the way it is." Pollard stood his ground.

"Then there's that big Sharps out there," said Fox. "Makes the men nervous."

"I got men out lookin' for him," said Pollard. "We'll get that son."

"Badger," Bradbury said. "Men like him opened this country. He was a friend of Carson and Bridger and Beckwourth."

"I'll open him up," Pollard promised. "It's that damn stone house worries me."

"Trevor," growled Crane. "Kovacs, a damn farmer. The Whelans, a couple bums from no place. Pig farmers. Women."

"And Buchanan," said Bradbury.

"Agh, you've turned against us," cried Crane. "Come on, let's get away from this. We got to figure somethin' out."

They went away toward the knoll. Two more wagons came through the woods, plodding along, bringing more gunners. Bradbury shook his head, watching them. Riffraff, saloon dregs, saddle bums, he thought. They were scraping the bottom of the barrel. The world had gone loco, and he sat in the middle of it, helpless.

He thought of Consuela and their children, of his *hacienda* and the money in the bank and the cattle roaming the range. He had enough, he had made it all the way. He wondered why he was here with these people formerly his friends and associates. It was a nightmare.

The fever was on, the people in the stone house had to be sacrificed. But for what? Fox and Crane were wealthy enough. Pollard had a fine job at the ranch. What had got into them all that they should strive to own the entire country, that they should hang Adam Day and burn out Trevor and come here to kill?

His stomach turned over. Now he knew he could not sleep even if he had the opportunity, even if there was not a rifleman watching him every moment.

The night went away. Badger came in at noon. He simply walked to the back door, the long rifle cradled. The mule was not in sight. Coco saw him first and blinked.

"Man, you IS a ghost."

"Y' larn out there," Badger told him." You don't want to be seen, then they don't see you."

"That's a trick I'd like to learn," said Coco. "They seen me too good." He was still hobbling, still bent to the aches of his ribs.

Amanda bustled with food for the mountain man. Raven came in and sat close to him. They seemed to be able to communicate without speech.

Buchanan asked, "How is it with them?"

"They still bringin' in men. They got a reg'lar army out there all right."

"If you got a notion, I'd admire to hear it."

"None whatsoever. 'Ceptin' you got a place, here, they got to get to it." He unslung a large leather pouch. Raven took it and removed various rootlike plants and leafy herbs. "Can you stay alive long enough, somethin's bound to give."

"Could you get the women out?" Buchanan asked.

"Might could after dark tonight."

Amanda said, "Not me. Not Jenny."

"Raven could go," said Buchanan. The Indian girl was already at the stove, separating the plants, scrutinizing them closely, working with a sharp paring knife. "She gets her medicine brewed, she can tell the others what to do. I don't see any reason a Crow gal should stick here."

The Kovacs looked stricken. Raven gave them a loving glance but was silent at her labor.

"Maybe I'm wrong," said Buchanan. He was already distraught about Jenny and Pieter. "It's up to her."

Badger ate. Buchanan was worried far more than he

would allow anyone to see. There were Cactus and Sutter, now talking together in one of the bedrooms. True, he had saved Sutter's life, but he knew the way these men thought —it was on his orders that Sutter went to the house and was wounded. Neither of them were reliable. And Badger . . . he was unpredictable, a man on his own, with his own philosophy.

The mountaineer was saying, "The good Lord don't want them people to prevail. Trouble is, sometimes He ain't lookin' down on you all. . . . Got to figure, He's got plenty to worry about all over the world."

"Never call on strangers when neighbors are near," suggested Buchanan.

Trevor came into the kitchen for a bite to eat. "Right-o. One does the best he can and accepts the Lord's help with humble gratitude." He looked at Buchanan. "Thorne's on the roof. I'll take him something to eat."

"They're quiet out there," Buchanan replied. "I don't like that any time."

A bullet sang its way through a window as if to prove him right. He did not like any of it. He went into the big room. Weevil was at a window with a rifle.

"They'll be comin' again tonight," said Weevil.

"Every night."

Cactus called from the bedroom. Buchanan went in and looked at them, Sutter with his leg bound but seemingly able to move around.

"Buchanan, we don't like this nohow."

"You forgot the Alamo already?"

"Maybe we don't have to run. Maybe we can palaver with 'em. Kovacs says they'll let the women go. That's a sign of somethin', ain't it?"

"It might have been. Now your boss is dead and a lot of them are dead. You don't hear them askin' for a parley."

Sutter said, "We might could all make a run for it after dark."

"That's been suggested," Buchanan told him. "Anything else on your minds?"

"We just don't like the odds. Ain't enough fighters in here. Just about everything's wrong."

"Uh-huh," said Buchanan. "You study on it. Then let me know what you decide."

"I don't like the way that broke-down wrangler and the nigger look at us," said Sutter.

"Seems like you're mighty sensitive," said Buchanan. "But I wouldn't mention it to them. They're kinda unhappy about bein' beat up and all."

He left the discontented pair and went up the ladder and onto the roof. He needed to be alone with his thoughts, and he needed action. He waited for a puff of smoke from the trees and took an offhand shot.

A man came tumbling down. There were savage yells, and a flurry of shots rang off the stone of the house. He emptied his rifle at the spots where they came from and heard howls of pain. The firing from the trees ceased.

Now they opened up from the knoll, which was far longer range. Still Buchanan persisted, not noticing the hog farmer who stretched alongside him, watching, eyes round. Elevating his sights, Buchanan poured lead atop the knoll. There was enough ammunition for a short siege, and he knew this one could not last long.

Then suddenly he desisted. There was no way to know if he was doing any damage on that faraway hill. He was taking out his anger and puzzlement by his action, and it was not doing any particular good.

Sonny Thorne said, "You sure put it to 'em, Mr. Buchanan."

"Uh-huh."

"I ain't sure I can hit a one of 'em. Pa shot at people in his time. I never did before now."

"Comes a time." He knew here was another less than hearty fighter. Yet Sonny had not refused duty at any moment.

"It keeps comin' back to me that you ain't got any stake here. It's just that you're mad at them for hangin' Adam and beatin' on your friend, the nigra and all."

"It's enough."

"It wouldn't be enough for me," said Thorne frankly.

The man could be right. Buchanan turned over and stared at the blue Wyoming sky, at the clouds, now white and fluffy, moving gently against the high heavens. "It's the way things are. Or the way they get to be." He tried to explain, then knew it wasn't any use. "We're here. We make a fight."

"Yessir. You mind now if I go down and get a bite in my belly? Just thinkin' about it all makes me hungry."

"Send Trevor up if he's ready," said Buchanan. He had to think, he had to work out defenses, a plan, something. Trevor was clever, he thought, maybe the Englishman could help. There were just too many guns out there and too little time to defend the house. He thought again of Durkin and his defiance and his misplaced bravery. It could happen to any of them who was not careful.

And it could happen from within. He clearly saw the danger there; he knew that people with the best intentions could not withstand the terrific strain of continuous bombardment.

He turned back to watch the trees and the marksmen who were concealed in them. They were beautiful trees, and now they were scarred with bullets, with climbing up into them . . . and falling down out of them. . . .

Trevor was speaking with Amanda when Sonny Thorne gave him Buchanan's message. He nodded, listening half to the woman, half to the murmur of voices in the bedroom where Sutter and Cactus spoke together.

Amanda was saying, "Buchanan seems to see it all clearly. It is the measure of the man."

"Ah, yes. He has been here and he has been there and he has profited by his coming and going, what?"

"Yes. He is here. He will be gone."

"You divined that. Women! Bless 'em."

"And damn them. According to their lights." She began to make a sandwich for Thorne.

"Oh. I say," he began, and paused. "I do know how it must have been for you. I mean, Adam burning as he did, eaten up with his ambition."

She said quietly, "It burned him that Bradbury and the other big ranchers looked down upon him. And . . . there were other factors, of course."

"Yes, quite. It was evident."

"Not to anyone else in Wyoming, I am sure," she said.

"When you left. Should have kept goin', you know. Wouldn't be in this mess, now, would you?"

"There is a principle here," she told him. "The land that was Adam's is now mine."

"You'll not live on it."

"No. But I must defend my right to it, to the farm, to everything. Maybe Adam was wrong-headed. He did not deserve to be lynched."

The rumble of conversation continued in the bedroom. Trevor said, "What one deserves and what one gets . . . ah, well . . ." He gestured. "Those two men. They'll bear watching. And Pieter, what of Pieter?"

"I agree about Durkin's men. And the Kovacs are not themselves. In shock, perhaps."

Trevor said, "I really had better speak with Buchanan. Excuse me, please?"

He smiled at her, then went up the ladder with his rifle. Amanda put the bread and meat in front of Thorne, wiped her hands on the apron she had borrowed, and went into the big room. Weevil was at one window. The other was unprotected for the nonce. Coco was reloading a rifle, gingerly but with precision.

"Guns," he muttered. "All the trouble comes with 'em."

"You're right," said Amanda.

He stared at her. "You the only one believes me."

"There's one small problem," she said. "If we had no guns, and they had all those people out there without guns . . . they could come and take us."

"But they couldn't shoot us."

"No," she said. "They would use rope."

Coco bowed his head. "Maybe you right, too. It's just I see so much harm done by the guns."

"Not the guns. The people who handle them." Then she was ashamed for having taken the tutorial stand with this gentle black giant. She asked, "Aren't you a champion?"

"I am the champion prizefighter of the entire West," said Coco. He straightened his back. He popped his eyes. "You know what? This champion couldn't stand up straight yesterday. That lil ole Indian gal, she said today it would be different. And it is!"

"Indians have their ways of healing," said Amanda. "Raven has a reputation in this country. Dan Badger seems to help her whenever he's needed."

"This here's a queer crowd," Coco said. He looked back into the kitchen where Raven and Badger were attending to the herbs and roots stewing on the stove. "Them two, they truly know somethin'. And that pair, the Whelans, they stick together like glue, don't they?"

"A queer crowd," she repeated. It was, indeed. "I guess it all comes down to Buchanan. Either he pulls us out of it or there'll be no crowd."

Coco said, "Tom will think of somethin'. He always does. Thing is. . . ." He paused.

"Yes?"

Coco spoke softly, "Ain't no guarantee some of us won't be hurt bad. Includin' Tom Buchanan."

"Yes. Of course." She went again to the kitchen. Neither Raven nor Badger spoke to her.

The Kovacses were in their bedroom, now vacated by Coco and Weevil. They sat close together, saying nothing.

Only the two cowboys talked, and Amanda could not quite distinguish what they were saying. She was afraid that it was something she should overhear and report to Buchanan.

She made more sandwiches and asked Sonny Thorne to take them out to the Whelans in the barn. Then she went back into the big room and stood beside the unguarded window with a rifle in her hands. She did not fire at anyone, but it made her feel better . . . useful . . . to stand there.

8

Bradbury was watching the sun fall toward the western mountain range, wondering if he would see it rise the next morning. A wagon driven by Toad Tanner and Dab Geer pulled in. There were half a dozen men aboard, singing, shouting, waving bottles. There were two barrels of whiskey in the wagon body.

Fox said, "Got it, didja?"

" 'Twarn't easy." Old Dab Geer scowled. "Them damn saloonkeepers wouldn't sell us none."

"Not even Noonan?"

"Not neither of 'em."

"You didn't cause trouble?"

"Hell, no." He motioned toward Tanner. "He 'membered the hotel. Just walked in and he'ped ourselves."

"Got it from ol' Weevil's place, huh?"

"You betcha. Had good whiskey, Weevil did, better'n the saloons. We watered one barrel some. Too good for them bums over there."

"Don't give 'em any 'til dark, you hear?" Fox said. "Just enough to stir 'em up for the charge."

"Be hard to keep 'em from it."

"Put a guard on it. And don't belt any more of it your own selves, neither."

"Got enough in us now, Boss."

The wagon lumbered away with its drunken load. Bradbury looked after it, disgusted.

"Damn fool mistake," he said. His eyes burned and he felt shaky, but he was awake. "Whiskey and war don't go together, no matter what anyone says."

Morgan Crane yelled, "You set there and run down every damn thing we do. By God, I don't know about you, Brad. By God, you ain't with us."

"And haven't been for some time." He was no longer frightened. He expected them to kill him sooner or later. There was always a guard lurking in the trees or sitting nearby. There had been no possible way he could have walked away.

"Shut up, Morgan," said Fox. "Let's go over and make sure Dab and Toad don't start pourin' rum."

They walked together through the trees. A rifleman nodded at them and sat watching Bradbury.

"Looks like he'll have to go," said Crane.

"Wait and see what happens when we get rid of them people down there."

"I don't cotton to the way he stares at us. Nemmine what he says, which is bad enough. He could turn on us, like we said, make a heap of trouble. He ain't fired a shot, y' know."

"He's with us. He's a member of the association," said Fox. "He's in it, all right."

"I still don't like the way he sets there, starin'."

"Fret about that later." They walked on to the knoll.

Bradbury sat on the log. He saw the guard in the woods. He surmised that Fox and Crane were discussing him. He was too weary to care at the moment. His spirits fell to new lows with each hour. He heard the sound of an approaching vehicle, which surprised him because the wagons were all at the scene of the battle now.

As the last rays of the sun flickered through the trees, he saw the carriage, pulled by a matched team. Miguel Carranza was driving. It was Bradbury's own equipage.

And seated beside Miguel was Consuela.

He cried out, "NO! Go back!"

The guard was coming from the trees. Miguel picked up a double-barreled shotgun and jumped to the ground. Consuela put a hand on the shoulder of her favorite driver and leaped lightly to earth. She went to her husband.

"Ah," she said. "You have not slept. You are weary."

"You got to get out of here. Dealer and Morgan, they've gone loco. It's dangerous here for you."

"And for you?" She patted his cheek.

Miguel was walking toward the guard. He showed white teeth in the failing light. He said, "You want some buckshot, *amigo?* No? Then keep your distance from my lady and the *señor.*"

The man said, "Hey, Mike, you know me, Sanders. I got orders, is all."

"Keep your orders away from us," Miguel told him.

"Hell, there's a hundred men up here'll make you yell uncle."

"When they do, you may come closer. Until then?"

"Okay, Mike. But I'm warnin' you."

Miguel shrugged and took a position between the guard and the Bradburys. She was sitting on the log now, and his head was on her shoulder. There were tears on his face.

She said, "The brave men talked in town. I sent Miguel to learn what he could. Then I knew I must come to you."

He said, "It's too late."

"We could drive off. Who is to stop us?"

"They'd send for us. Make it look like an accident. You got to go, Consuela. You can't stay here."

"So. We cannot escape. I see it. But I will not go."

"You got to, I tell you!"

She gestured. "Those women down there. Are they not with their husbands? Did you not ask them to leave?"

He nodded.

"In the town they know that, also. They talk. It will never be comfortable for Dealer Fox nor Morgan Crane in Buffalo again. If they had arms and a leader, I believe they would come here and fight."

"Is there a chance? . . ."

"No. Your former friends have cleaned out the ammunition. There is no one to lead them. The telegraph wire is down. They sent a rider, but it will be too late for him to bring help. No, you are right. We will remain here."

"But not you!"

"Oh, yes, my dear. Me, Consuela." She fumbled in her dress, produced an ugly, short-barreled revolver. "Remember this? You gave it to me to use, if needed, while you were away. It was long ago when we were young."

"I remember." He did, indeed. His mind, stretched by the hours without sleep, by fasting because he was afraid food would induce slumber, ran whirling back to those days. His wife pregnant or caring for young children, himself in a honky-tonk or a barroom or up against a card table; yes, he remembered. She had never complained, she had been a devoted mother and wife. "You just can't fight 'em. There's too many. They got rifles. And now they got booze."

"I know. They stole it from the hotel." She was utterly calm. "Miguel, the basket, please?"

Not taking his eyes from the guard, Miguel went to the carriage and brought a basket to them. She lifted a clean white towel and displayed cold turkey and ham and canned peaches and a bottle of wine.

Now he was famished. With Miguel and Consuela standing guard on their part, he might eat and sleep and regain the resolution and intelligence he needed.

"Thanks, Consuela," he said humbly. "I guess I got to get strength. I don't want to die. Maybe . . . maybe we can work out something. If only Dealer and Morgan were their own selves . . . But they ain't. They're crazy to kill. It does things to men."

"They are fools."

He was reaching for the delicate viands. "Yes, they're damn fools. But they got the guns. They got the men to shoot 'em. It's a dead-end proposition."

"We're alive," she said. "Eat. Sip the wine. Then we'll watch while you sleep."

She composed herself on the log. Miguel flashed her a comforting grin. She adjusted the revolver in her ample lap where it would be handy in case of need.

Out on the prairie, the stars began to twinkle in a sky now clear. The hills lay northward, toward the town and county of Sheridan. Beyond there was an encampment of Crows, people of peace.

The tall mule carried double with ease. Raven's arms were warm around the waist of Dan Badger.

He said, "The raven is a talkin' bird, little daughter. But you do not talk to me."

"I must think." They spoke in the Crow tongue.

He reined in the mule. They slid down to earth and faced each other in the twilight.

He said, "I couldn't leave you there."

Now she switched to the proper English she had learned in the school. "They are so good to me. Even their religion is good, much like our own. The Great Father . . . you know."

"I know some, not all."

"They have no children of their own."

" 'Tain't our problem. I don't want you there when the end comes."

"You believe it will be a bad end."

"It can't be much else, now, can it? Too many guns outside."

"I could be of help."

He said, "Child, you're my daughter, never forget. Nobody knows but old Chief Chinook. Nobody knows how they kilt her when she was comin' to me. Damn Blackfoot."

"You have sent many of them over."

"I did, daughter. I did. But I stopped. Figgered I'd kilt enough of 'em. Never did know if I got the right bunch."

"It is the Indian way."

"Yes. And now it is the Injun way to repay the Kovacs."

"Yes. You will stay."

"Won't be long now. You take the mule and go home."

"Will they accept me, father?"

"The old chief will accept you."

"Chinook."

" 'Tain't his Injun name, y' know. I give it to him durin' a winter thaw when he saved the tribe by movin' 'em to shelter before the change came."

"My grandfather?"

"Yes."

She said, "You have told me the way." She hesitated, her emotions showing for the first time. "Pieter and Jenny. They are so good."

"Mighty fine folks." He shifted the Sharps rifle. "I'll do what I kin."

"It will not be enough."

"Don't reckon so." There was no use to try and lie to her, she was too direct, too intelligent.

"I will think of them."

"You do that."

He gave her a hand, and she pulled up her short skirt and settled into the saddle. She looked down at him. "I know it was best you left me with them. Still . . ."

"No way for me t' settle down. I come out here when I was a boy. I married the mountains afore I married your ma. We all did, them that came early. Shoot, honey, I was an agin' buck when you was born. I don't know how many breeds I got on women before then. Don't fret on me."

"Those bad people that attack the Kovacs. I do not like to think of them and what will happen."

"A whole lot of 'em will come to Jesus afore it does

happen," he told her. He patted the rifle. "It's a bright night. I'll take a heap of 'em over."

"It is not enough."

"Don't fret, I say. Go home and learn the good ways of Chinook. You're a Crow girl, y' hear me?"

"I am half white."

"It don't show a bit on you. Chinook won't give it a thought. Grandchildren are special to Injuns."

"I remember."

"Then go. The fight'll begin anytime now. I got to pay for what the Kovacs did for us."

"I do not like it, father." She sat erect in the saddle, staring at the stars.

He slapped the mule on the flank. "EEyaw, outa here," he roared. The big animal bolted, with the girl in the saddle bent to the task of controlling it.

Badger watched until he could no longer see them. Her mother had been the last and the best of his wives. She was the only offspring that he knew to be alive and well.

In those early days, the only way he could have survived alone in the wilderness was to make friends with the Indians. They had all done so, Beckwourth, Carson, Bridger, Williams, all but Jed Smith, and he had met his finish at the end of a lance, him and his Bible. Sometimes even being married into a tribe didn't help, either, when they got drunk on whatever was their local brew and went berserk.

But old Chinook had sold the girl for a fine horse, ten blankets, a rifle, a Bowie knife, and a tin bathtub that one of his wives used for cooking fat dog—and was well pleased with the bargain. He was a good man, Chinook, and he could fight if he had to. Now he was peaceable, the army had taken away his guns, and the people moved with the seasons, not living their old life but not on a reservation, either. The army was tolerant because of Chinook. Raven would adopt her Indian name and become one of them, which was right and proper, because look what was happening to her foster parents, the Kovacs, in this world of the white man.

Badger walked. He had walked all over God's West in

his time. His stride was as natural as breathing and even now, in his old age, he was tireless and swift. There was a duty to be carried out. The Kovacs might die, in spite of Buchanan and his smart thinking, but Badger would claim many an eye for a tooth. His pouch was full of the bullets he had poured and made into cartridges for the old Sharps, and he knew how to use it better than anyone alive. And when it came to the end and he had to get within range, there was the Green River knife and a short-handled, sharp tomahawk in his belt.

"EEyaw," he said and walked a little faster.

Jenny Kovacs sat on a bench in the big front room of her house and wept, the tears running down her broad cheeks as Pieter tried ineffectually to wipe them away. Amanda stood before her, seeking words of comfort. Weevil crouched at a window, silent, as was Coco at the long table.

"Is gone," Jenny cried. "My house. Look at it! Now my little girl, my baby."

Cactus and Sutter came from the bedroom. Sutter was using a straightbacked chair for a crutch. Each wore a six-gun, and each carried a rifle. Amanda backed warily against the wall.

Unnoticed, Sonny Thorne stood transfixed in the closet, preparing to go to the roof to join Buchanan and Trevor. The Whelans were still in the barn standing guard.

Pieter looked at nothing. "Is so."

"I know what you mean," said Cactus softly. "Me and Sutter, we been talkin'."

"There ain't no way," Sutter said. "There just ain't no way outa this."

"Is so," said Pieter Kovacs, his face stony.

"It's your house." Cactus brought his rifle around to bear upon Weevil. Sutter covered Coco. "You want to quit, you got the say."

"We can talk to 'em out there," Sutter said. "We know them. They know us."

"If they want Buchanan . . . give 'em Buchanan," said

Cactus. "Give 'em the Whelans and Trevor and all. It ain't our fight."

"You're crazy!" cried Amanda.

"Just lower your voice, lady," Cactus warned. "Anybody makes a big holler gets it right here and now. This thing's gone far enough. No use to run—but we can talk terms to Bradbury and them."

"That's right," Sutter said. "We can get outa this."

Sonny Thorne suddenly started up the ladder. Cactus heard him. In two moves, the cowboy was in the closet and swinging the butt of his rifle.

Sonny fell without a sound. Cactus dragged him away from the foot of the ladder and shoved him into a corner of the room. Jenny and Pieter watched without emotion. Amanda gasped. Coco made a move, then stopped. Weevil did not stir from his place by the window. A random shot came flying in and thunked into a hanging mattress.

Cactus said, "Okay with you, Kovacs? We talk to 'em?"

Jenny answered for the two of them. "Talk. Bring back my baby girl. Stop this killing."

Cactus said, "Sure thing." He went into the closet and called in a normal tone of voice, "Buchanan. Time to switch, ain't it?"

"Comin' down. You and Thorne can handle it up here," Buchanan answered.

Now Cactus held the rifle steady, facing the ladder. Amanda bit her lip. Sutter was watching them, rifle in hand, the other hand on his revolver. Coco leaned against the table. Weevil started to bring his rifle around, was stopped by a gesture from Sutter.

It was Trevor who dropped lightly from the ladder. Cactus stuck the muzzle of the rifle in his face. Trevor ducked and sprang into the room. He saw Sutter, saw the situation and cried out, "Buchanan, watch out!"

Sutter fired a shot. Trevor went down. Amanda screamed.

Buchanan landed on his feet, knees bent, revolver drawn. Cactus had his finger on the trigger of the rifle.

Buchanan said, "Pull . . . and you're dead."

Cactus held fast. "We want to talk."

"Not to me," said Buchanan. "Put down that gun or say your prayers."

From his corner, Weevil drawled, "Better do like the man says. You start somethin' and we'll blow the joint apart."

Coco moved, painfully but with purpose. He came up behind Sutter. He kicked the chair away and seized the rifle. Sutter groaned as he hit the floor.

Cactus cried, "The Kovacs wanta quit. We got a right. It's their place." He lowered the rifle and backed into the room and stood beside Sutter, helping the other cowboy to his feet. "Ask them. We want to talk to Bradbury and them."

Amanda had flown to the side of Trevor. He grinned at her. "Bad shot, what? Just a shoulder."

"I didn't want to kill nobody," said Sutter. "I coulda got him dead center."

"Decent of you, old boy," said Trevor.

Buchanan said, "So you want to talk to them? Kovacs?"

"Is so." He was dull-faced, as though not involved in the action. "Me and Jenny."

"Should we let Cactus and Sutter show us how it's done?" Buchanan asked gently.

"Any way it can be done," Jenny said. "My baby is gone. My house is ruin."

"But not blown up. Not yet," Buchanan said. Then he shrugged. "You want to talk to them, go ahead."

"Gimme a white flag, anything. I'll go out there," said Cactus. "Them people know me."

Jenny Kovacs arose. She went to a chest of drawers and took out a spotless white sheet. "God bless," she said, handing it to Cactus. She did not look at Buchanan.

Amanda said, "Come with me, Trevor." She led him to the kitchen and began to remove his jacket. She called to Buchanan, "I do not agree with this."

"Uh-huh," said Buchanan. He watched Cactus attach the sheet to his rifle barrel. He motioned Coco and Weevil to stay away from the door. Sutter had regained his chair and was following Cactus.

Cactus yanked back the heavy bar. The door swung open. He stuck the rifle out and waved it. Night was falling fast, but there was an answer from the forest. Cactus and Sutter went out into the open.

It was Jigger Dorn and Dealer Fox and Morgan Crane who appeared from the shelter of the trees. They walked only a few steps and stopped.

Fox called, "Where's Buchanan?"

"Never mind him," Cactus replied. "We wanta talk terms. We wanta know if you'll let us all go."

"Listen at the cowpoke," said Crane.

"It's some kinda trick," Jigger Dorn said, grinning like a death's head. "Get 'em."

Buchanan grabbed a rifle from the table. Shots rang out. Dorn was firing his revolver. Buchanan got off one shot, then Coco slammed the door.

Buchanan ran to the window. Dorn was down. The others had already dashed back to safety. Every gun from the trees and from the knoll began to shoot. Lead poured at the house. Cactus and Sutter lay in a pool of blood.

Buchanan said dully, "You might want to see, Pieter. You might want to learn what good it does to talk to those people out there."

He turned away, sick at heart. Now they would be coming in force, he was certain of that. Trevor was hurt. The Kovacses, looking wan and lost, crept away to their bedroom. He went to where Sonny Thorne lay.

He knelt and felt for a heartbeat. There was none. The young hog farmer was dead. Cactus and Sutter had done their damage before paying the price.

He went to the deep closet in which he had placed the box of dynamite. They would come with the wagons, he knew. They had discovered a way to have some protection as they attacked.

He opened the box and selected three sticks. He tied them together with wire. He fingered a detonating cap. It was necessary to soften the dynamite to insert the cap the way he wanted it.

He struck a taper and lit the stub of a candle he had found in the barn. He held it steady. One wrong move and he would blow up the house, and at the moment, it mattered a bit less to him than it had before.

The moment passed. He inserted the cap. He attached a short piece of the fuse.

He remained in the closet. He had six caps, he wanted to make a half-dozen bombs. He was not altogether certain that he had done the job properly. Once, he thought he might have gone too far. Once, he was afraid he might set off a spark and finish everything right then and there.

He persisted. It was going to be a bad night, as bad as any he had ever known. He drew a deep breath and went out to the kitchen.

Trevor's right shoulder was bandaged, the healing Indian poultice was in place. Amanda was once more getting food together. Her face was pale and she did not smile.

Trevor said, "Good bit of luck I'm ambidextrous. Shoot with either hand, you know?"

"You'll get your chance." Buchanan dropped heavily into a chair. Coco came and sat beside him. "It'll be a doozer tonight, I promise you that."

"The Whelans?" Trevor was cool.

"I'll talk to them. If the attack is on the house, we'll bring 'em in. We'll need every gun. We'll need Amanda and Coco to reload."

"I can shoot," Amanda said flatly. "If I must, I can shoot at them."

"Just keep the gun loaded," said Buchanan. He looked at Coco. "Think you could get up on the roof with me?"

"I can do it."

"I got me a bit of an idea," said Buchanan.

"If they come all the way, with more than one wagon . . ."

"I'm countin' on it."

He looked at Pieter and Jenny, clinging to one another, completely lost, now, hopeless, abandoned. He went to stand before them.

"It's just too late," he said kindly. "It's gone too far. You saw what happened, we lost three guns tryin' to talk to those people out there."

They did not reply. He sighed and went to the back

door. Amanda was waiting, knowing he was heading for the barn and the Whelans.

She said, "You tried. Don't blame yourself."

"It is their house," he said. "Their barn, their land. Maybe we should've made the fight somewhere else. But it had to be made. More and more, I know it had to be made."

She reached for his hand. "Win or lose, we'll make the fight."

He returned the pressure. Then he ran for the barn with food in his pockets. The Whelans were staunch, he thought. He would remain with them for a while. He needed to know what the enemy was planning. He felt looser in the barn, from which he might venture a scout again if necessary.

Dealer Fox stood in a wagon behind the knoll and dipped out whiskey rations. He was guarded by Tanner and Geer, both well plied with liquor. Tin cups were filled, emptied, passed around.

Morgan Crane had his own bottle. He was frustrated, angry. "Got to git goin'," he repeated over and over. "Got to git them bastards where I want 'em."

Sime Pollard, notably sober, stared at the men. "Only way this bunch'll get us there is if they're stone drunk. I got the shooters in the rear guard where they might do some good."

"Git 'em all up there," roared Crane. "Git every damn man up there."

Pollard said, "No."

"You tellin' me?" Crane whirled around.

From the wagon Fox said, "He's right, Morgan. We agreed; he's in charge of deployin' the men."

"I dunno," shouted Crane. "You and him. You let that greaser Miguel scare you off. You let Brad and his woman set there, no tellin' what they're up to. I dunno but it's time somebody else took charge here."

"Like you?" asked Fox.

"Like this affair's got to be finished tonight," Crane declared. "We still got a hundred men. If they can't get down there and wipe out that lousy little crew of rustlers and turncoats and whatnot, then there's somethin' damn wrong."

"Buchanan," muttered Pollard. "That's what's been wrong all along. Buchanan."

Fox continued to dish out seconds and thirds to those who wanted the whiskey. If they became wild enough, he thought, they would charge through any gunfire and reach the windows of the house and throw in the torches he had ready for them. Once the place was afire the rats would have to depart the house. Then it would be all over in a minute or two, and the burying could begin and the story embroidered for public release.

Now one of the crew began to lead a group in song, *"Mine eyes have seen the glory of the coming of the Lord . . ."*

It was not tuneful, but it was loud and it raised the hackles of men who had sympathized with the South in 1861. A long, screaming Rebel yell mounted to the oblivious stars, and the dissidents were shouting, *"'Way down south in the land of cotton, old times there are not forgotten, look away, look away, look away, Dixieland . . ."*

In a jiffy, they were facing each other, brandishing knives, fists, tin cups. Fox had stacked the rifles, but one man drew a hideout short gun.

Morgan Crane drove among them swinging his fists. Pollard buffaloed the man with the gun. They milled in a confused welter of violence.

Fox said, "Fire over their heads. Damn, they'll kill each other off."

Tanner and Geer obliged. Bullets flew close enough to the embattled men to cause them to duck. Pollard laid out another man.

Fox shouted, "That damn war's long since over. This one right here's what you're bein' paid for—better money than you ever got from the gov'ment."

They were quiet under the lash. Someone hollered, "More whiskey, that's the game, boys."

Fox doled it out in smaller quantities. It had been a narrow escape. Mob spirit had to be controlled, directed. The trouble was that the best of the shooters had died in the earlier, brave attempts on the house. He prayed for another hour, and then it would be over. All but taking care of Bradbury and his wife, he added to himself. That was another matter. . . .

Miguel said to the guard, "We will move. For what it is worth, we could kill you now if we must."

The guard said, "Sime'll kill me if you try to git away."

"We are not running," said Miguel.

They watched each other like two bulldogs, ready to fight if necessary. The Bradburys walked to where they could see what was going on beyond the knoll.

They watched and listened to the howls, then Bradbury said, "A mob. A drunken mob."

"It started with a lynching," she reminded him.

"Curse the day I hired Sime Pollard."

"He's a good cattleman. The association began this other thing that brought us here."

"I know. I know," he groaned. "I see it all now. I see it when it's too late."

Fox was handing out the torches and giving instructions. He lit one and held it high over the scene. The flickering flame threw a macabre glow over the motley crew. Geer and Tanner still held their guns at ready. Pollard lounged, scornful, indifferent. Crane waved his arms as usual, shouting, exhorting them to "go down there and git it over with."

"They will go and face the guns from those people in that house?" queried Miguel, unbelieving.

"They hired out to do just that," said Bradbury. "It's charge the house or be shot down by Pollard and Geer and Tanner and Crane. And maybe Fox, I dunno. Dealer ain't real brave, but the madness is on 'em."

She took his arm and led him gently away, back to the comparative safety of the glade in the woods. She said, "But you regained your sanity. It will be remembered."

"Maybe," he said dejectedly. "I'm part of it. No way out. Pollard was there when they lynched Adam Day."

"You were not there. We'll think of a way. The children must never believe you're part of it."

They sat on the fallen tree trunk. She poured the last of the wine. Miguel and the guard faced one another, squatting, alert. The sound of the mob grew louder. The reflected glow of torches lit the sky behind the knoll.

Bradbury fingered his rifle. Their time would come, he thought. He was weak for want of sleep. His head nodded.

Consuela put an arm around him, pulled him close. He tried to remain awake but could not. He slept fitfully, moaning, twisting, turning. She managed to get his head down into her lap, taking the rifle and placing it at her side. It was a long time since they had been this close.

Buchanan talked with the Whelans as they ate. The noise from the other side of the knoll was increasing.

"Drunk," said Rob Whelan with satisfaction. "Never did see a drunk man could hit a bull in the ass with a shovel."

"Rob," Fay protested. "You promised not to talk like that."

"It's a time for anything rough," Rob said. "It's like the old days, some."

"But not quite?" Buchanan asked.

"No, not quite, you bet," Fay answered for her husband. "We was always alone."

"Until we got together," Rob said. A figure showed itself against the skyline, and Whelan fired his rifle offhand. The man fell backwards.

Buchanan said, "Heard a lot about you and your shootin'. I see nobody was prevaricatin'."

"That's what started the trouble," Rob said. "I was too good too young."

"Leastways you know what's goin' on," Buchanan told him. "There's Cactus and Sutter layin' out there. They didn't know."

"Neither did Durkin," Fay said. "Always tryin' to be the big man."

"All his life," Buchanan agreed. "Thing is, if those people over yonder do make a rush, we haven't got enough guns to stop 'em."

"Take a lot of 'em along, though," Rob said.

"That ain't good enough," protested Fay. "We come this far, we want to keep goin' awhile."

"That's what's needed," Buchanan said. "You got to want it real bad. If we knew which way they were comin', we could do better. Cover me."

He was off and running before they could reply. He went westward, describing a circle, again aiming to get behind the knoll. It was easy to see that the action would come from there. The sharpshooters in the trees were not about to charge across open ground to the house.

He was amazed that there were no patrols out. Any military skirmish was unsafe unless patrols were maintained. He was able to crawl within a couple of hundred yards of the enemy force. He could distinguish the leaders by the light of the torches. The mood of the men was plain to see; they were singing and dancing and waving their arms. He knew at once that Fox and the others had passed out the booze.

It was enough to learn at this time. It meant a wild and feckless charge by the numbers, the drunks little caring whether they lived or died. He began his retreat.

In a moment or two, he knew he was not alone on the prairie. He sank behind a clump of furze and waited, all his senses attuned to sound or movement.

Time passed. There was danger that the attack would begin, leaving him out here when he was needed indoors. But his plainsmanship was sound; he knew the first motion on his part might make him a target. He held his breath. He was prone, facing into the slight breeze in the direction from which he imagined he had heard the sound.

A hand clamped upon his shoulder.

He rolled over, cocking the rifle, but a soft voice said, "Now, son. Now, now."

"Badger," he whispered. "Dang you. I might've shot you."

The mountain man chuckled. "You're good, Buchanan. But not that good."

Buchanan relaxed. "Reckon you're right there. I'd bet no other man in the country could come up on me like this."

"It's the way we was." Badger held the Sharps rifle in his hands, peering at the yelling people behind the hill. "I might could pick off one or two. Wouldn't do much good."

"No. Best to wait. . . . Did the Indian girl go home?"

"You agin it?"

"Not so long as she can make it."

"Muley'll git her home. You know about Chinook and his people?"

"Can't say I do, 'ceptin' they're peaceable."

"They turned in all their guns. The army don't bother 'em none. Says they're a good example. They use bow and arrow, fish, hunt a little, grow some maize. She'll be safe with old Chinook."

There was no good in telling of Trevor's wound or the despair of the Kovacs', which had encouraged the two cowboys to rebel and attempt to parley. . . . Buchanan put it out of his mind for the present. "You could've gone with her."

"Yep. Thought on it, too. Old codger like me, should be thinkin' of the grave. Just couldn't take another gun away. This land belongs to them folks."

"The land." Buchanan sighed, beginning to gather himself for the trek back to warn the defenders that a drunken mob was about to attack. "You think of the land. Me, I think about the people. It's a big subject, maybe too big to augur on."

"The Lord will provide," said Badger. "Do you get goin' now. I'l be out here somewhere or t'other."

He melted into the darkness—but it was not that dark, and he had the gift of the invisible cloak, Buchanan thought, making his own way toward the Kovacs' barn. When he was a boy, his mother had regaled him with such marvelous tales—the seven league boots—he never had figured out how long was a league. . . . He came close enough to rise, and he ran the rest of the way to the safety of the stable, calling out to the Whelans.

It was none too soon. The howls were growing louder, the torches threw an eerie light. They came first in a wagon, as Buchanan had imagined.

The Whelans came from the shelter of the barn. Buchanan knelt between them. They could see the charge forming.

Rob said, "They must be drunk to the boots. Givin' us light to shoot by."

"They're drunk," Buchanan said. "Try to stop the wagon, they must have more damn dynamite."

Fay Whelan stretched out on the ground. "They'll have to run it right on over me. The fools, I could feel sorry for 'em."

"Don't," said her husband. "They hired to kill us."

They had only three rifles. Buchanan wondered who was on the roof of the house and if the range would be good and how many wild drunks would be racing down the hill. He placed a box of cartridges beside him.

He said, "Rob, you start firin' when ready. Fay, you let him get off six shots. Then you start."

"Yeah. Then I can reload while you two are still shootin'," said Rob.

"If they get too close, it'll have to be the sixguns," said Buchanan. "I haven't got much faith in 'em, myself."

"Great in a saloon." Rob grinned. "Get it out fast, stick it in their ribs. That's what a Colt's for."

"Worse the luck," Fay said. "Killed more fools than the epizootic plague."

They were the coolest couple Buchanan had ever met. Something could be advanced in favor of early adversity, he pondered, watching the attack form atop the knoll. The Whelans had seen hard times for so long that nothing could faze them. They had fought for no stakes at all. Now, at least, they had something for which to risk their lives.

He thought of taking them back into the barn. The problem was that a direct fire could not be laid down from that position. They would be firing from a doorway, one at a time. To ward off this charge would be difficult enough as it was.

Rob said, "Reckon I got 'em, now."

The wagon was rolling, men trying to conceal themselves behind it and alongside it, not succeeding too well. The yells became clearer, the long Rebel, the Yankee hoot, a few Indian warwhoops.

"They aimin' to scare us to death?" asked Fay Whelan.

At that moment, Rob began shooting. One man went down. There was a miss. He swore heartily and elevated his sights. A second man fell.

As he let off the sixth shot, Fay began firing. Buchanan watched closely, whistled beneath his breath. Fay was bringing them down as if they were tenpins, aiming for the legs of the men behind the wagon.

He joined in the attack. The screams of the wounded began to mingle with the shouts of the drunken attackers. Men ran clear of the wagon, frenzied, unwitting.

The solid boom of the Sharps rifle came from the west. It sounded like the clap of doom, it struck to the very souls of the more sober attackers. Buchanan emptied his magazine, and now Rob was reloaded and firing again.

A small group of men came crazed down past the wagon, and now it was plain that the dead and wounded had piled up under the rear wheels, stopping its progress. The Sharps sounded again and another victim fell.

Buchanan said, "Let's take out this bunch."

Fay and Rob began to shoot at the charging group. Buchanan joined in, also aiming low, wanting to stop them without killing them if possible. The men fell and rolled and still yowled their crazy song of defiance. These were the most drunken, he thought, these were the poor fools who did not fully realize what they were doing.

Once more, the Sharps rifle of Dan Badger sent its zooming message across the prairie. And there was silence.

The charge was broken. Wounded men tried to crawl back up the hill. There were curses and groans, and all the song and all the fiery spirit had collapsed and was no more.

Buchanan said, "Okay, back to the barn."

The three of them withdrew from their position. Shots were coming now, with better aim, as sober gunners took over from the top of the knoll.

Inside the barn Rob said, "Didn't see hide nor hair of Dealer nor Morgan nor Brad. Not Pollard, neither, none of them."

"No," said Buchanan. "No chance, not on a suicide run like that."

"Maybe not never," Fay said. "But they stopped just in time. I'm runnin' low on bullets."

Buchanan said, "Want to make a run for the house, you two?"

"Some hot soup wouldn't hurt," Rob confessed. "And I got this here little nick."

Fay gasped but did not cry out. "Where?"

"Just in the ribs, like. C'mon, we'll go in and take a look at it."

Buchanan watched them go. Rob was walking straight and she was following. They broke for the house, and he staggered. She braced him, an arm about him. Amanda opened the door, and they made it to safety.

Safety for the moment, Buchanan added to himself. There would be more tonight. It was early. By dawn, they would come again, certainly more shrewdly, with better planning behind the attack. There had to be some brains among them. It was standard procedure that the hotheads and dummies would have their say. Proven wrong—or killed—they would shrink into the background, and the men who knew how to fight this kind of a battle would take over.

He settled down to watch and think . . . and wait. It was always the hardest part, the waiting.

They were loading the wounded into the wagons. Men went down and rescued their friends, at first fearful of attack from the defenders, then with boldness as no one tried to prevent them. The men with the shovels went back to the trench to bury the dead.

Sime Pollard said, "No way you're gonna get them to try that again. Forget the barn."

Dealer Fox raged, "If they'd just kept on goin'. That was Buchanan out there, I'll bet my life."

"Your life wasn't on the line," Pollard told him.

"You expect me and Morgan to go down there?" screamed Dealer Fox. "We're payin' for people to do that."

"Dead men can't collect," said Pollard.

"We ain't scared," Crane insisted. "It just ain't our job whilst we can hire men."

Pollard looked at Tanner and Geer. They shrugged, nodding agreement to his leadership. The foreman of the Bar-B turned his attention to the dead, the wounded, those who were left of the bunch behind the knoll. Torches burned low, there was a queasy expression on the faces of too many of them.

Pollard said, "So far it's been a dumb play. You want to listen to good sense or don't you?"

"We're the boss here," said Fox, but he had followed Pollard's inquiring survey, and his voice was weak.

"Then you go ahead and run it without Toad and Geer and me," said Pollard indifferently. "My boss seems to have lost interest. I'd as soon quit."

"Now, wait," said Fox. "That ain't no way to talk. Let's all have a touch of that good whiskey and talk things over."

"Don't need booze," said Pollard. "We can augur right here and now."

Geer and Tanner moved in. The three of them were formidable, and Fox realized that, under the circumstances, anything could happen both to him and to Crane, who was as drunk as any of them. His devious mind described a huge circle.

"Okay, Sime. Reckon you're right. Reckon we ain't done any good 'til now." His voice was oily, he managed a grin. "Reckon we'll have to go in the next time. Show the men we're with 'em all the way."

"The dynamite," said Pollard. "We got to use it. Wagons and the dynamite."

"Can we do that?"

"I can do it," said Pollard. "I know about dynamite."

Morgan Crane was emptying the first barrel, staggering, mouthing obscenities to the watching men. Fox turned away from him.

"Sime?"

"Yep."

"You pull it out. Then we'll talk real business."

"Like about Brad?"

"He's through, you know that. And look at Morgan. Only you and me are makin' any sense."

"You figurin' to do away with Brad?"

"It'll be an accident. Like when they drive out in their carriage. Maybe one of your sticks of dynamite?"

"Mebbe."

"Then you run the Bar-B."

Pollard shook his head. "Then I OWN the Bar-B."

"Now, Sime don't be a hawg."

"I own it. I been a drover all my life. Now you all got me into this. And I know where I stand. I'll take care of Toad and Dab. But I get to own Bar-B."

Fox looked at the hard-faced lean foreman, saw danger, saw raw ambition. He also saw intelligence, possibly a way to get through this dangerous setup.

He dissimulated. "Well . . . if that's the way it has to be."

"That's the only way," Pollard said coldly.

"But first we got to finish this job clean."

"We let 'em sweat. Come sunup, we hit."

"You're the boss."

"Right," said Pollard. "And you go down there with us, you and Morgan."

"Agreed."

"Sure. Agreed. And I'm goin' to see you do it." Pollard's laugh was without mirth.

"Okay, Sime. It's your wagon."

"Wagons. Me and Toad and Dab. We'll convince the men. We blow up the house from the wagons. Forget the damn barn, we only lose at the barn."

"And they'll expect us to hit there."

"You're catchin' on, Dealer." Pollard walked away.

There went a really dangerous man, Fox thought. Now he would have to think real hard. He could, of course, start down on the attack. There was bound to be confusion. He could slip away to safety.

No use to worry about Morgan. He had slid down to the ground, his head against a wagon wheel, snoring. Many of the men were sleeping, either from exhaustion or because of the booze.

He walked around the knoll and up to where he could look into the glade. The Bradburys slept against each other, but Miguel was awake and on guard with the shotgun. The man left to watch them was also partially awake. It didn't matter right now.

Dealer Fox looked up at the sky. He took a deep breath. He suddenly felt more alone than he had ever been before.

9

Buchanan awakened with the touch of Coco's hand upon his arm. He started. The smell of dawn was on the air. He was still in the barn.

Coco said, "The trees, Tom. They beginnin' to move over in the trees."

"Who's on the roof?"

"Them Whelans. He got a bullet in the side, but he climb up there with her. His wife. They mighty tough people, Tom."

"Mighty good people." He rinsed off his face at the

water bucket, from which they had sipped water during all the previous day and night. "I had a dream."

"Good dream or bad dream?"

"I don't know. It told me they wouldn't try the barn, here, next time."

"Shoot, didn't need no dream for that. They got knocked out twice, tryin' it here."

"But we need cover here." He brushed the last vestige of sleep from his eyes. "Trevor. How's his arm?"

"He been shootin'. Him and Weevil. At them trees."

"Miz Day?"

"She fixin' food and all. She loadin' guns with me. Maybe she got an hour sleep or so."

"The Kovacs?"

"They just set. They'd do anything to stop it, I do believe. When the little old Injun gal went away, they was finished."

"Uh-huh. And how do you feel?"

Coco brightened. "Little old Injun gal, she done wonders for me. It hurts . . . but I can navigate."

"So we got Weevil and Trevor and the Whelans, four guns. Maybe Amanda to fire a few shots. We got Badger outside. Then there's you and me."

"I can't shoot no gun."

"I know." He weighed the odds in his mind. "We better get to the house before there's light to shoot us by."

"Me and Amanda, we brought out the other corpus," said Coco, pointing. "Put him there with his daddy. Them other two, couldn't get to them. They're in the yard where they fell."

"Amanda?"

"The Whelans was on the roof. Trevor's hurt. Weevil's got but one leg. The Kovacs, they just set and stare." Coco spread his muscular, huge hands. "Wasn't for my ribs, I'd be all right."

"You keep 'em bandaged tight. And come on, now." Buchanan led the way to the house in the deceptive light that precedes dawn. It was the time when all energies are low, when people cannot see the light after a long night. It was the lowest ebb of fortune.

Amanda held the door. There was coffee on the stove and a pot of hot gruel, a porridge of sorts. Buchanan swallowed the coffee, admiring the widow's coolness and courage.

A bullet came through one of the windows, missed a hanging mattress, skipped off the stone wall, whistled into the kitchen. Amanda pushed back a strand of hair as it clanked against the stove and fell harmless to the floor. There were dark hollows beneath her eyes.

"Pieter and Jenny have given up," she said, ignoring the flight of the deadly hunk of lead. "Weevil is exhausted. Trevor's wound is infected in spite of the Indian herbs . . . I may have applied them wrong."

Buchanan said, "Won't take a long while to decide it now. One way or another."

"I can see only one way," she said, low-voiced. "There are just too many of them."

"That ain't the way to look at it." He went to the closet where he had manufactured his dynamite bombs and began to stow them in his pockets. She followed him.

"We began this together." She stood very close to him. "Mainly because of me you're in it."

"Nope," he told her. "Just a notion of mine that people shouldn't be lynched. Nor beaten and jailed, like they did Coco and Weevil."

"Still, we were in it from the start."

"Uh-huh." He looked down at her from his considerable height. "I call it good company, no matter how it goes."

The tired eyes of the woman flashed. "Yes. Good company. Don't forget that, Buchanan."

"Couldn't forget it," he told her. "You been somebody else, all the way. Keep it that way."

"Isn't there anything I can do? To help?"

"Just what you been doin'," he said.

She nodded. She was disheveled and not too clean, but there was a wild beauty about her. "It seems we've been here forever. Doing what we can. All the killing. I can't quite take it in, not yet."

"Don't try," he advised her. He walked into the big

front room, death in every pocket of his jacket and pants, death in his revolver, in his rifle. He looked at Trevor, then at Weevil.

"I'm bringin' down the Whelans," he said. "Coco and me, we'll take the roof."

"The barn?" Trevor was flushed in the light of the sheltered lamp. "What of the barn?"

"They'll be comin' right to us this time," Buchanan said. "It figures. They got the wagons. They'll have learned somethin' by now."

"Learned?"

"How to use 'em. The fools have died. Pollard's no dummy. This'll be the big one."

Weevil said, "Dynamite. They got to have more'n you took away from the first wagon."

"Right," said Buchanan. "So we'll need all the fire power here. If they go the other way, then the Whelans can swing out and I'll be with 'em."

"If they get close enough, we're goners," said Weevil.

"You might say it that way," Buchanan agreed.

"By God, I'd rather take it outdoors."

"You might get the chance, too." Buchanan went into the bedroom and looked at the owners of the stone house.

Pieter and Jenny still sat on the bed, close together. Their eyes were devoid of emotion, now. Jenny fingered a rosary, her lips moving.

Buchanan said, "Sorry about all the damage. But the buildings are solid, nothin' can happen to them."

"Is lost our lil girl," said Pieter.

"She'll be back."

"No." He was positive. "Her people no fight, kill."

"Uh-huh. Reckon most of your fight was for her." Buchanan shook his head sorrowfully. "Once into it, there's no way to stop. You saw them cowboys get killed. Talk stops after the first shot is fired. That's just the way it is."

"It can never be right again. If we live . . . we go," said Pieter Kovacs. "Is not worth it."

"I'm right sorry. You got a nice spread here." He left them. Words could do nothing at this time, and he knew the first rays of morning would soon spread into the

Wyoming sky. Some people were like that, brave as brave until that certain nerve was exposed. With them, it was the Indian girl they had reared, who had become so important to them. They should have left with her, he thought now. It would have been better all around if they had gone to the far hills and the Crow tribe.

He beckoned to Coco, and they climbed the ladder to the roof. Bullets flew above their heads as they crawled to the parapet.

Rob Whelan said, "They are sure settin' up somethin'."

"You note their target."

"Yeah. The house."

"Like we said before. You want to go back to the barn?"

"You got a good reason?" Whelan scowled, dubious. "Seems like we need all the guns right here."

"Look at it this way: if they hit here full force, a flankin' fire from the barn'll come in mighty handy. And if Badger's still out there, it might do a heap of good."

Fay Whelan said, "You ain't lettin' me out because I'm a woman, are you, Buchanan?"

Buchanan grinned. "Beggin' your pardon, but you haven't been actin' girlish since this whizbang began."

"Now, that's the nicest thing's been said to me in a long time," she said.

"You totin' that dynamite?" asked Rob.

"Figured it might be useful." Buchanan stretched out and removed two bombs from his pants pocket. "Me and Coco, we can handle this. You might leave an extra rifle, pick up another downstairs."

"It makes sense," said Rob, eyeing the stick of dynamite with distrust. "I don't know nothin' about that stuff."

"Come on, honey," said Fay. "I'll bet Buchanan knows."

He had, indeed, experienced an occasion when explosives had saved some lives under different circumstances. It did not give him too much confidence about these crude, homemade bombs. But he thought of the war wagons that the enemy had for its attack and took out the rest of the bombs, stowing them close to the parapet where they would be safe from a random bullet. Coco was reloading the rifle left behind by Whelan.

Buchanan said, "This won't be a picnic, you know that."

"Don't expect a picnic," Coco said. "Hope that little old Injun gal got clean away, is all."

"She did. I talked to Badger."

"Then they didn't get the old man."

They went to the ladder. Coco was awkward making the climb, favoring his broken ribs, using the power of his long arms to haul himself up. Buchanan carried the rifles and ammunition. They snaked their way under constant attack from the trees. Darkness prevented sharp marksmanship, but the first tendrils of dawn were spreading in the east.

Buchanan said, "Damn trouble is those people. They got the nubby on us."

"Guns," said Coco. "Stinkin' guns."

Buchanan picked a spot from which much of the firing seemed to be emanating. He watched for dots of red, then shot into a dim mass of thick branches. For a couple of moments, nothing happened. He persisted.

Bodies made sounds, and there were hoarse cries as men fell from their perches. Limbs creaked and splintered. Heavier fire came at once from other sections of the small forest.

"They must be about ready to hit us," Buchanan said. "Keep that dynamite handy. And be careful."

"Careful? I treat it like thin-shelled, white hen's eggs," Coco said.

"Be ready with the matches."

"If I can hold 'em steady. This here stuff's worse'n guns. It goes off, it kills us all."

"Don't let it go off. Hold it ready, is all."

"I'm as ready as I'll ever be," Coco told him. "Thing is, what am I ready for?"

Buchanan had no answer. He could only wait. He believed the attack would come at the house. If it did not, he would transfer the dynamite and his body and Coco's to the barn. It was once more a matter of waiting and sweating and hoping he was correct.

Dealer Fox moved away from the main body at the knoll. It was just before dawn, and the torches flickered. In his pocket was a capped stick of dynamite attached to a very short fuse, like a firecracker. He had thought about this all night, and his courage was screwed up to its highest pitch.

Pollard, he thought, would be next. He could handle Morgan Crane and the others. Bradbury, then Pollard, that was the way it had to be.

He came to the glade. He spoke to the guard, sending him to join the main body. Bradbury sat with the rifle loosely held in his hands. Consuela stood, expressionless. Miguel held the shotgun ready.

Fox said, "Conny, Brad. This is goin' to be it. This is goin' to blow 'em out. Pollard's got it figured."

"Women and all?" asked Bradbury.

"They had their chance. It's got to be clean, now. Then . . . well, Pollard's makin' demands. He wants the Bar-B."

"Pollard? He wants to own the Bar-B?"

"He hired those gunners. He's got Tanner and Geer on his side. What can I do?"

"I wouldn't expect you to do anything," said Bradbury heavily. Consuela moved, her hand hidden in the voluminous folds of her skirt. "Nor Morgan."

"We been friends a long time. Morgan's drunk, he don't count. No, I got to look out for you best I can."

"Look out for us? How?"

"The carriage. Miguel can drive you. Take off and keep goin' until you hear from me," Fox said rapidly.

"And where would we go to be safe?"

"Sheridan . . . Cheyenne. . . . Just don't say nothin', lay low. I'll do what I can here."

Miguel said in Spanish, "Do not believe him. He lies."

"Hush. Do as he says," Consuela answered in the same language.

Miguel hesitated, then went for the horses. Consuela smiled at Dealer Fox.

"It is good of you to allow us to escape. Morgan and Pollard would have killed us."

"Yes. They spoke of it."

"And made it look like an accident," she went on. Miguel was hitching up the team.

"That was the idea," said Fox. "I couldn't hold still for that, after all we been through."

"All the years buildin' the country," said Bradbury. He put the rifle into the carriage. "So you're goin' to finish 'em down there, are you?"

"Sime figured it all out. We got the men in the trees, there, to keep 'em holed up. With the wagons and some dynamite . . . it'll be over in a few minutes."

Miguel climbed to the seat and picked up the reins. Fox came a little closer in the dim light. "Goodbye for a while. You can depend on it, I'll be in touch."

"Yeah," said Bradbury. He turned and helped Consuela into the carriage. Then he suddenly wheeled and faced Fox.

In his eagerness, Fox had taken the dynamite stick from his pocket and was reaching for a taper. Perhaps he thought the uncertain light would conceal his intent. Perhaps his nerve had nearly given out, and he had to make a move.

Bradbury went for his holster gun. He hadn't drawn in years, in fact he had never been fast. Fox struck the match.

Consuela's hand came from her wide skirt. She had not relinquished the revolver. She lifted it and fired.

Fox spun around. Bradbury's Colt cleared. He shot Fox through the head. The match fell atop the slumping body, burned a moment, flickered out with the life of the man.

Consuela said, "I saw it in his eyes. And so did you, husband."

"Yes. I saw it."

Miguel said, "That man, he could not tell a truth. Should we go now?"

They looked at one another. They shook their heads.

Bradbury said, "No. Pollard's alive. Pollard wants the Bar-B. Pollard!"

"Morgan's alive," said Consuela. "He will join with Pollard."

Miguel said, "I think we must kill them, then."

There was a sound behind them, a man coughed. They whirled and stared into the huge muzzle of a Sharps rifle. Dan Badger was watching them.

"Miz Bradbury, gents," said the mountain man, "I seen it all. Might've shot him myself. Aim to do a little shootin' afore this is over. Mought advise you all. Stay close, folley me. Could be a help."

"But they'll kill those people in the Kovacs' house."

"Could be. In that case . . . we'll all go with 'em." The deepset eyes blazed at them. None of the three cared to deny him.

Buchanan squinted at the sky. It was pink, and it would be red, Wyoming red. All the signs pointed to a hot day. He lay there on the roof, pinned down by constant firing from the trees. It was at great risk that he kept any kind of watch on the knoll from whence he knew the attack had to come.

He said to Coco, "Don't lift your head. Believe me. Stay down low and wait until I tell you to move."

"Don't you worry about me. Them bullets sound like a mess of hornets to me."

"They kill quicker."

"I don't even like hornets. I been bit by hornets."

"They got to begin," Buchanan muttered. "The Whelans will see 'em first, no doubt. If we hear the Whelans begin to shoot, we'll know."

"Yeah, but what good'll that do if you can't see?"

"Just have to risk it." He removed his hat and put it on the muzzle of the rifle. He raised it slowly above the parapet. It was promptly riddled with bullets.

"They got enough light to line up on us. They never did have that many good shooters in the trees. Means they got somethin' real hot planned for us this time."

Coco said, "Don't say that. It gets any hotter, I ain't goin' to be here. I'll be melted clean away."

Buchanan himself was sweating. The women below and

the nature of the fight—for the rights of citizens—combined to make this the most meaningful battle of his life on the frontier. And it seemed to be a fight he could not win.

Perhaps he had been wrong to stake out the roof. He could not make a move so long as the sharpshooters in the trees concentrated their fire upon him. Maybe he should go down and join the Whelans in the barn.

Some instinct of battle had made him choose this stand. Even now it nagged at him, held him there, his hat full of bullet holes, depending upon his ears and his highly developed sense of imminent and dangerous action to guide him.

He heard the sound of firing from the barn. The Whelans were involved. He managed a one-eyed peek above the parapet.

There were two wagons already started down the incline from the top of the hill. Men were pushing, also clinging to the sides, dangling their legs to provide no targets for the Whelans. A part detached itself and went toward the barn, firing rifles, ready with revolvers, and Buchanan prayed for the brave former outlaw and his saloon-girl wife.

There were men in the first wagon. He recognized Tanner and Geer. He saw them pick up sticks of dynamite, just like those that were beside him. Both sides had arrived at the same conclusion; explosives would turn the tide, he realized.

The fire from the trees continued. He showed an eye, and a bullet barely missed him. It was dawn now, the sun rising bright, the clouds scudding before its bright gleam. Buchanan did not bother to reach for his rifle. He would be dead before he could get in a shot.

The first wagon was coming closer. Geer was lighting the fuse on one of the dynamite bombs. Buchanan knew it would be directed at the house, where Trevor and Weevil were firing as fast as they could, knocking over a man here, hitting a leg there, doing their best to stop the inexorable advance of the wagons.

Buchanan found his own three-stick bomb. He looked

at Coco and said, "This might be it for me. Can you light the rest of 'em and throw 'em down?"

"If they get you, I'll be able to do it." Coco's eyes were bright with tears. "Lemme try it first? You can shoot if I don't make it."

"Not your turn," said Buchanan. "My bombs, I made 'em." He winked and grinned at his friend.

Then he got to his knees. He fully expected at least one bullet to strike him then and there. He lit the fuse with his match. He reached back and threw for the wagon, full arm, with all his strength. Then he ducked. He was astounded to find himself unhurt.

He managed to pop his head back up. He saw his bomb descend upon the first wagon just as Geer tried to throw at the house. There was a shattering explosion. The wagon blew apart. Geer, Tanner, and the men with them vanished.

The echoes had not died when Buchanan heard another sound. It was the booming of the Sharps rifle. The shooting from the trees had magically ceased. Buchanan let out a whoop.

The second wagon came on. Pollard and Morgan Crane stood in the body. Pollard swung and a sputtering bomb described a parabola. It was going to land inside the house, through one of the high narrow windows.

It was ticketed for the death of all within. It could kill Coco and Buchanan on the roof. It could be the end.

Buchanan lunged. Reaching far out over the edge of the parapet, he thrust out a long arm.

His eye was sure, he fielded the bomb. Quickly he let it go, flinging it back from when it came.

Coco threw himself across Buchanan's legs. With one hand, he grabbed at the collar of the shirt, holding it for one moment, feeling it rip. Then he had shifted position.

The bomb went off. It had not quite reached the wagon. Pollard and Crane leaped free.

Buchanan yelled, "Let me down, Coco. Easy does it."

Coco's ribs were caving in. He made one huge effort. He swung Buchanan around, got hold of his wrists. The big man hung a moment, like a pendulum. Shots narrowly missed him. Then Coco let go and Buchanan dropped to earth.

He landed on his feet. He drew his revolver in the same instant.

Pollard was firing. Buchanan did not move. He sent a bullet crashing through the cowman's heart. He spun and saw Morgan Crane with a rifle pointed. He shot Crane clean out of the body of the wagon in which he had been hiding.

The Sharps boomed again. Men came running from the trees with their hands over their heads. Brown men drew the bowstrings and let loose arrows. There were shouts of "We surrender!"

Buchanan stared in disbelief. Around the corner of the barn came the Whelans. They were surrounded and backed by Indians with quivers of arrows and long hunting bows.

A quiet fell upon the battle scene. A pony and a tall mule trotted into the clearing before the house, daintily picking their way among the dead and wounded. Raven rode the mule. On the back of the spotted pony was a small, wizened man who wore the headdress of a chieftain.

Badger came swinging down from the trees, followed by other Indians. Consuela and Brad Bradbury preceded the mountain man.

The siege was broken. The fight was ended, all the leaders disposed of, the issue settled for this time and place. Buchanan drew a deep breath.

"Well, Colonel?"

Badger spoke up. "He got Dealer Fox. I seen it. They was holdin' him under guard."

Consuela pleaded, "He was not responsible for the lynching of Adam Day. You know he sent for you, trying to prevent bloodshed."

"I know he acted like a damn fool back there in town," said Buchanan.

"I admit it," said Bradbury. His face contorted. "I'll do anything I can, Tom. Anything."

"I'm no judge," Buchanan told him. He looked at Badger. "Raven brought the Crow?"

"She did. 'Twarn't my idee." Worry creased his brow. "They ain't supposed to fight, y' know. Could make big trouble for them."

Chinook rode his spotted pony in close, spoke in his native language to Badger.

The mountain man said, "Anything for his grand-daughter, he says. Because she loves the Kovacses."

The tiny old chief sat tall on the saddle blanket. Buchanan looked thoughtfully around. He brightened.

"Those prisoners," he commanded. "See that they collect all the arrows. Every last one, you hear?"

"Yes, sir," said Miguel, who still clutched his shotgun.

"Whelan, take charge there. See that they take care of their own wounded. Get rid of every evidence that there was an Indian around here. Understand?"

"They saved us back there." Fay pointed to the barn. "We were goners when they rode in."

"Uh-huh." He turned back to Bradbury. "You never saw an Indian, did you, Colonel?"

Bradbury said steadily, "I'll swear to that along with plenty of other things."

"Uh-huh. Other things. Amanda Day. The house and grounds belongin' to the Kovacses. The Whelan ranch. You can't bring back Durkin nor his men nor the hog farmers. But you can see to their property if they got relatives."

"I swear to see to it all," said Bradbury. "I'll take care of the association, too. This here was all wrong. Maybe I seen it too late, but I know it now."

"He knows," said Consuela. "On my children's heads I swear to help him."

Buchanan said, "I believe you. As to the rest, it's up to the people. It ain't goin' to be easy. These things ain't easy forgotten. If I was you, I'd start right now."

"Got a carriage," said Bradbury. "Maybe we should get back to town and get the telegraph wire up and all."

"And Weevil's hotel. Don't forget that you owe him."

"If it takes every cow I own, Tom."

Buchanan bowed to Consuela and watched them follow the loyal Miguel back up to the trees from which so much harm had come.

Badger said, "Looks like we made Christians of 'em."

"Brad wasn't a bad man," Buchanan said. "Trouble is, people get so much, they scare easy."

"And pick up with evil companions," Badger said. "The Lord moves in mysterious ways, his miracles to perform."

Buchanan looked at Chinook, the chief of the Crow tribe. "Reckon you're right. He moved the Crow down here in time to clear out the sharpshooters. They had me tied down."

Badger spoke to Chinook. The old man's lined face cracked in a broad grin. "People good to Indian girl. Indians good to people. We go, now. No been here?"

"No been here," Buchanan said. " 'Ceptin' I'll be comin' your way soon. Like maybe there's some little thing I can do." Whelan and Fay were distributing the used arrows.

Chinook lifted a hand. His braves rode to form a circle. Still smiling, the little chief turned toward the mountains and led them into the growing heat of the morning.

Badger said, "Knowed him many a long year. I'll just say howdy to Raven. Then I'll be moseyin' along."

They went into the house. Jenny Kovacs was holding Raven in her arms. Trevor and Weevil were washing gunpowder from faces and hands in the kitchen. Pieter Kovacs stood, stone-faced, surveying the damage to his house. Coco came to Buchanan. Amanda followed, her face shining, her color restored.

Buchanan said, "Coco saved the whole shebang. I'd have broke my fool neck and maybe blown up the joint if he hadn't grabbed me."

"That Injun gal. Minute she come around, the voodoo worked," Coco said.

Buchanan said, "Holy cow!"

"What?"

"That dynamite! On the roof."

Coco showed all of his white teeth. "Don't you worry. I done brought that down with me. See?"

He began to pull the bombs out of his pocket. Buchanan let out another yelp.

Coco had neglected to remove the caps and fuses.

Buchanan gathered them lovingly and ran outdoors. Trevor lounged out, his arm in a sling.

"I say, old boy. Bit of a mess, now, wasn't it?"

The disarmed prisoners, in fear for their lives, were cleaning up. Mangled bodies were being carried to the trench behind the knoll. Drivers took wagons full of wounded toward the town. Buchanan removed the fuses with great care.

"A lot of work to do," he said. "You ready to tell a heap of lies to the association?"

"If the truth won't serve."

"You and Brad."

"Yes, I understand. We'll work it out, make reparations, all that. Rebuild. . . . We all have a stake in this country, what?"

"I don't know how Kovacs is goin' to take it. Or the Whelans. This was a bad time. Best you should sorta promise them help."

"Will they believe me?"

Buchanan disarmed the last sticks of dynamite. "You got a way with you. Reckon you can do it if you want to bad enough."

Buchanan made a neat stack of the dynamite sticks. He handed them to Trevor. "Could be useful for buildin' as well as tearin' down," he suggested. "Got to think of it thataway."

He went back to the house. Amanda was waiting for him. They walked into the kitchen, she proferred a huge sandwich.

"I thought you might be hungry."

He accepted it. "You always guess right."

"So it's over."

"This part is over."

"And you?"

"Me?" He sat down. Raven and the Kovacses and the Englishman were in a consultation. Fay Whelan came in, listened, joined them. Coco and Weevil listened with interest. "I'll be movin' on."

"Where to?"

"Well." He bit into the sandwich and considered. She

was in earnest, she wanted to know. He swallowed. "First off, to town. Weevil's got a bath, hot water and all, if they didn't tear it down. Kinda rest up a couple days, maybe. See how things begin to work out."

She asked abruptly, "You wouldn't be interested in taking over my place?"

"Your place? A farm?" He shook his head. "Not even if it was Bradbury's Bar-B. No. Me and Coco, we move around, separate, meet up. It's a life."

"No women, Buchanan?" She stared at him boldly.

"Women don't cotton to a wanderin' man. They want . . . well, like they want a farmer."

She did not flinch. "I'm no farm woman. I learned that. I learned it the bitter way."

Buchanan said, "When you get organized and all, I'll be in town. Maybe I can help you sell the farm. Or somethin'."

She said, "Will you? I like that." She smiled. "I particularly like that last."

"Somethin'?"

"Something," she said. She went to where Trevor was laying the plans for reparations that Bradbury would have to carry through.

Coco said, "Can we leave now?"

"Catch up a couple horses," Buchanan told him. He finished the sandwich with one more huge bite.

Coco said, "You know what?"

"I got an idea."

"You have, huh?"

"Sure. Every time we get through one of these rangdoodles you want to fight me. Only this time you can't because you got your ribs busted."

"That ain't all I was thinkin'. It's about that little old Injun gal. Reckon it'd be okay for me to come by sometime and look her up?"

"Why not?"

Coco said contentedly, "That's just what I thought. Why not? Okay, let's get them hosses."

Buchanan led the way out the back door. There was nothing left for him to do here at this place. It had been a

rough time, but he had done what he could, and it had
ended well enough, as well as could be expected. The
country would continue to open up, there would be other
wars, other problems, but his part was played, the curtain
was down. He needed a bath, sleep, a day or two of rest.
He needed a good hot meal, properly cooked.

As to Amanda, he would let that rest. He was a peaceable man, and she was strong-willed. Dead game but awful
strong. A school teacher. Maybe she should go back to
San Francisco like she had planned. Maybe he would see
her there sometime.

He had nothing more to say to the others. He took
down two saddles from the corral rail where they had
somehow remained through the entire siege. It was time to
ride. The free life lay ahead. Tomorrow would always be
another adventure.

BIG NEW BESTSELLERS
FROM FAWCETT GOLD MEDAL